Surrea

NEAL PETERSEN

Cover Design: Deirdre Wallis

Paperback-Press
an imprint of A & S Publishing
A & S Holmes, Inc.

.

ISBN-13: 978-1-945669-45-3

DEDICATION

To the love of my life. I miss her more than I can
put into words.

Sherri Lee Laramore-Petersen
12/4/1962 - 4/25/2015

ACKNOWLEDGMENTS

To my late brother Doug and his wife Rocky Power, thank you for your considerable help in getting this story where it is today. May you both RIP.

Sharon Kizziah-Holmes and Paperback-Press, thanks for believing in me and my story. Your support and expertise in the publishing process means a lot to me.

Thank you to Kathleen Garnsey and Norma Eaton for your editing skills. I know it was a challenge but you did an awesome job.

CHAPTER ONE

Finders Keepers

I woke to a large wet tongue caressing my face and there was an uncomfortable pressure on my chest. I turned to release the pressure, opened my eyes and looked into my best friend's face staring incessantly into mine. "Ok, Doc, hang on."

"Rowlf," Doc answered back. He slipped off the bed and landed head first on the floor in his usual graceful manner. Shaking his head, he looked up at me as if it was entirely my fault.

Doc, a four-year-old German Shepherd stood nearly three feet at the shoulder. His color was mainly black, with a tan spot thrown in randomly for color. Otherwise, the only marking on him was a perfect white "T" on his upper chest. Doctor Tronopolis Kaledja is the name I gave him when I bought him at nine weeks old. Since his proper name was too long to call him by, I nicknamed him Doc.

I got out of bed and glanced at the clock. It was a good hour and a half before I would normally get up. "Oh, Doc, I'm going to have to break you of this."

There was no sense in lying back down, for two reasons; one, once I was awake, I could not get back to sleep, and two, even if I could, Doc would not let me. I slipped on my pants and proceeded to let Doc out the kitchen door into the backyard so he could relieve himself. I then headed for the bathroom so I could do likewise. By the time I got back to the kitchen, Doc was scratching at the door. I let him in and began looking through the cupboard and fridge for breakfast.

"What sounds good today, Doc? Bacon and eggs maybe?"

"Rowlf."

What dog would turn down bacon and eggs? Doc wagged his tail and watched my every move in anticipation. I opened one cupboard after another. "And what will you have, Beef Pride or Beef Pride?"

"Rowlf, Rowlf."

He knew very well which cupboard was *his*. Out of habit, I fed Doc first then proceeded to make my breakfast. After scarfing down our meals and cleaning up, I let Doc back outside for his morning romp. I then went to take a shower.

Standing in front of a clouded mirror, I said frankly to a very opaque surface, "I know you're in there, Thomas Franklin Brown." I combed my short *business cut* blond hair and kept staring into the misty mirror, trying to see my blue eyes. Being thirty-five years old, six foot three, two hundred and seventy pounds, I always considered myself as a somewhat handsome man, even though you could not tell by my love life. I had never had a lasting relationship and was currently unattached.

I slid my class ring, which I always took off to take a shower, back on my right index finger, put my watch on my left wrist, slipped on my sweat pants and a sweatshirt, and then went for my daily jog.

As always, I went out the back door. "Side Doc," I said in the tone I always used for a command. Doc, being very obedient, never required me to give the same command twice, took his place on my right side and followed me out the gate.

Roughly five miles and forty minutes later, we returned home. Another quick shower before I dressed for work. I looked at the clock.

"Six forty-eight, forty-two minutes before I leave for work and it's your fault Doc. Oh well, I guess we might as well make the best of it."

I grabbed the Frisbee off the top shelf of my entertainment stand where I kept it so Doc would not get a hold of it. When I made a dash for the back-door, Doc tried to grab it out of my hand. Flinging the door open, I threw it toward the fence. Doc flew by me and nearly knocked me over in the process.

Before it could hit the fence, Doc zeroed in like an expert marksman eyeing his target. All four paws left the ground and with the grace of an elephant trying to balance itself on a high wire, missed the Frisbee and smacked into the fence. The Frisbee nonchalantly floated lazily down to land in front of Doc's nose.

Recovering quickly from the mishap, Doc grabbed the Frisbee and proceeded to take the whole escapade out on it quite violently.

"Here," I commanded, before I saw another seven bucks get torn apart. "Sit on it," I said when I grabbed hold of the Frisbee. "Drop." Doc reluctantly relinquished his hold.

Again, the Frisbee went flying with Doc merrily in pursuit. This went on for nearly half an hour, till it was almost time for me to leave for work. "Time to pack it up Doc, off to work we go." I put the Frisbee back on its shelf and noticed Doc had that unmistakable look of a child whose toy had been stolen by the neighborhood bully. "We'll play later."

Glancing at the clock, it read 7:22 a.m., just eight minutes before I had to leave. I walked into the bedroom, placed my stopwatch around my neck by its twenty-eight-inch chain, and grabbed my tote bag, which had my street clothes, a pair of tennis shoes and Doc's leash inside.

"Here, Doc," I commanded as I went out the front door. This was quite unnecessary, since Doc followed me everywhere I went, unless he was tied up or told to stay. I opened the passenger door to my Classic '62 Chevy Biscayne. Doc, like a robotic arm placing a bolt in its hole, slid into his *rightful place* in the passenger seat. Closing the passenger door, I went around and got in.

During the twenty-minute drive to the *Trim and Fit* Fitness Center, a job that kept you fit, was a job most guys my age would love to have, so I really was fortunate. I considered myself lucky to have a job I not only enjoyed but would allow me to take Doc in with me since he could easily climb the five-foot fence in the backyard.

The last time I left him in the house by himself, it looked like a cross between ten spies looking for microfilm and a police raid looking for hidden drugs. I still think he had to have some help from *the little people* or something, because somehow, he managed to move a big enough pile of various items close enough to the shelf where my last Frisbee lay hidden and succeeded in getting it down. I can only imagine how much more havoc *Hurricane Doc* would have inflicted upon my humble abode if it had not been for that poor shredded Frisbee.

I pulled into the parking lot, found a space way in the back where I always parked and secured the car for the day. Doc and I crossed the lot and entered the fitness center through the main entrance. "Hi, Marcie."

"Hi, Tom, hi, Doc." Marcie waved. "Oh Tom, Jill wants to see you in her office before you start class."

"What does she want?"

The phone rang and she just shrugged her shoulders while she answered the phone.

I walked down the hall and knocked on Jill's office door. I studied the plaque on her door that read *Jill A. Humphrey, Manager*, and thought someday I would like to see it read *Thomas F.*

Brown.

Marcie's polite phone voice filtered down the hall, "Trim and Fit Fitness Center, may I help you?" At the same time a voice that sounded like it came from a heavyweight boxer instead of a woman, came resounding through the closed door.

"Come in."

I opened the door and Doc and I stepped in.

"Oh, hi Tom. Hi Doc." She smiled. I have something you might be interested in."

"What is it?"

She held up an old bottle. To some it probably would have looked like a piece of trash, but to me it was an ancient relic.

"I know you collect old items and I thought you might be interested in this."

"Where did it come from?" I heard my own voice sound like a ten-year-old boy who just got his first bicycle.

"I found it yesterday in a pile of dirt next to the hole they're digging in my back yard for the swimming pool."

She handed it to me and I looked it over carefully. I held it up to the light and gently tapped it with my finger. My best estimate was that it was around two hundred years old.

"I need to get to work; I'm going to put this in my car first. This is a great find. Thanks for thinking about me. I really appreciate it."

"You're welcome. I certainly didn't know what to do with a dirty old bottle." She laughed. "Now go and get to work."

"Thanks again." Doc and I jogged back outside

and put the bottle in my car, then hurried back to the gym. Five people were already waiting for the eight-thirty class to start.

The entire day, all I could think about was getting home to examine the strange bottle that had fallen into my hands. Since it was almost completely caked with dirt, I really did not know where it came from or what it truly looked like.

It was four forty-five p.m., only fifteen more minutes before my workday ended, when one of my oldest friends came in with a buddy of his I had never met before. "Hi, Jake. It's been a long time since I saw you last."

"Hey, Tom old buddy. How 'ya doing, man? I'd like 'ya to meet someone. This is Chris, a good friend of mine."

"Nice to meet you, Chris." I held my hand out so we could shake.

"Nice to meet you."

Chris grabbed hold of my hand and gave the appropriate handshake.

"And this is Doc," Jake stated.

"Say hello, Doc." Doc sat and put his paw out for Chris who bent over and gently grabbed Doc's paw in his hand. He shook it while giggling like a child seeing his first clown.

"So, have you beaten your record yet?" Jake asked.

"Last month I finally benched 352."

"Pounds?" Chris stared in astonishment.

Jake slapped me on the back. "Yeah, Tom here is a regular Hercules!"

It was three minutes till five and the bottle in my

car seemed to be calling to me. I was very anxious to get it home, wash it and take a good look at it. "Well, it's my time to go home and I have some important business to attend to. I apologize. It's so good to see you Jake, and to meet you Chris."

"I mainly brought Chris in to sign him up, so we'll be seeing you around a lot from now on. Maybe we'll get together soon and reminisce about the good old days? See you later, old buddy."

"It's a date my friend. Side, Doc." I waved and headed for the locker room. Chris said something I did not catch while I moved away, but I heard Jake say, "He's also a third-degree black belt." Normally I enjoyed talking about that, but I wanted to get home right now. There would be plenty of time to talk to Chris and Jake later.

Thirty-five minutes after I left Jake and Chris' company, I was viewing the dirt-encrusted bottle in my kitchen like one views a rare and precious gem. The first thing I had to determine was whether or not it would fall apart if I tried to clean the exterior dirt off.

After careful scrutiny, I felt confident enough to clean it. I lined my sink with sponges and made sure there was no way the bottle could accidentally come in contact with the stainless-steel surface. I laid the bottle down on my make shift sifter and slowly sprayed it down with the sprayer attachment I had bought for this very purpose, careful not to get the interior dirt wet. I was finally rewarded for my arduous work. After about an hour, I sat at my kitchen table with a magnifying glass and studied my newest treasure inch by inch.

Being a Friday night, and since I had Saturday and Sunday off, I could devote my entire weekend to my new toy. It was now 10:20 p.m. I usually went to bed between ten and eleven, but tonight I felt wide-awake with excitement.

I grabbed three reference books, one entitled *Ancient Indian Artifacts from A to Z*, another *American Antiques*, and the third, *North American Relics*.

The bottle's substance eluded me; if I did not know better I would say it was made out of metal. It was definitely not clay or porcelain. I could not see any cracks in the surface. It was almost completely covered with hieroglyphics I had never seen before. On the side in the center, was a circle that looked like it was pressed in when it was made. By the shape of it and the way the neck flared out at the end, it was probably a wine decanter.

I started going through my books to try and figure out the age of it, even though I thought it could not be of American or English origin, I went through that book first. Nothing even close, however, I expected this. *Ancient Indian Artifacts* came next and I had the same results. I searched the confines of the third book's pages. It was arranged in chronological order and started with items fifty or so years old to relics from the caveman era.

While I thumbed through the pages, exhaustion started to overcome me, and my mind began to wander, thinking about the bottle's possible origins, especially how it got in Jill's backyard. Then I snapped back to what I was doing when something caught my eye. My attention was drawn to a bowl.

My heart leapt. I grabbed my bottle and searched until I found the symbol I was looking for. I held it next to the picture and carefully compared the symbol on the bowl to the one on my bottle. They were a perfect match. The description read: *Possibly a ceremonial bowl, found in Canada in 1952, the bowl was believed to belong to an unknown North American Indian tribe of roving nomads. The hieroglyphics are of an unknown origin, dated seven hundred years old. Possible related finds pages 203, 207.*

I turned to page 203 and my heart pounded with excitement. I viewed the page and saw a knife with more inscriptions listed. My heart jumped into my throat. The top row of symbols around my bottle matched the ones across the knife perfectly, and they were in the same order! I read the description under the picture of the knife. *Considered a ceremonial knife, possibly used by the high priest, it was found in California in 1973. The knife was believed to belong to an unknown North American Indian tribe of roving nomads. The hieroglyphics are of an unknown origin, dated seven hundred to seven hundred and fifty years old. Possible related finds pages 200, 207.*

I quickly turned to page 207 and found my bottle. *Possibly a ceremonial flask, found in England in 1904, disappeared during World War II, was never found. The flask was believed to belong to an unknown North American Indian tribe of roving nomads and it is unclear how it made its way to England. The hieroglyphics are of an unknown origin, dated seven hundred fifty to eight hundred years old. Possible related finds pages 200, 203.*

How did it end up in Springfield, Missouri? Something was missing in this picture. Then I realized the circle in my bottle was not in the one in the picture. "Now, how did you get in there?" The odds that two identical bottles, with the exception of the strange circle, being made in that time period would be astounding and I knew it.

I decided to clean the inside of the bottle. It took me nearly three relentless hours. It was now four-fifteen in the morning and time had finally taken its toll on my weary mind.

I put the bottle on the table without thinking and called Doc, who had been sleeping on the kitchen floor most of the night. He got up while I walked out of the kitchen. I reached for the light and turned to see Doc, who was still half asleep, walk into one of the table legs.

Being a rather flimsy table, it shook violently and the bottle, which I had foolishly put on the edge, toppled off and headed towards the linoleum floor.

"No!" I cried, loud enough to wake the neighbors and made a diving leap for it. I was too far away from it to even get close, but that did not stop my enormous effort to reach it before it hit the floor. Nevertheless, of course, it did and I didn't.

I watched it fly through the air in slow motion and quickly dove to save my beautiful, antique keepsake. Poor Doc, heard me scream a familiar word and when I leapt in his direction he turned and ran straight into the wall with his tail between his legs. My body slammed onto the floor. I was too late. I watched in horror while the precious bottle shattered into a thousand pieces.

I dragged myself up off the floor and started to sweep up the pieces. I carefully inspected the floor to make sure I had not missed any fragments and piled them on the kitchen counter. That was when I noticed the ring.

It was very heavy and I wondered if it might be gold. It had six stones spaced evenly around it. Two looked like rubies, two more like diamonds and the last two emeralds. Each stone was square cut and roughly four carats in size. The inside of it was also inscribed with symbols similar to the ones on the bottle.

I took the ring and placed one of the stones that looked like a diamond against a glass and using a very small amount of pressure, ran it around the entire circumference. I took the glass and lightly tapped the inside of it around the groove the stone had made with the handle of a butter knife. Then I barely hit the side of the sink with the glass, and the bottom of the glass fell onto the sponges. It looked like I had used a bottle cutter on it.

I picked the ring back up and noticed it was roughly the same finger size as my class ring. Without thinking, I slipped it on my left index finger. It slid on easily and felt like a perfect fit. It was as good a place as any to keep it until I could have it appraised. I turned the kitchen light off and headed to bed.

"Here, Doc." I slid into bed and eyed the clock. July 2, 5:59 a.m. Then it clicked to six o'clock and I closed my eyes. I may have lost the bottle, but at least I had a valuable ring. Anything that old had to be real.

Somewhere between consciousness and dreaming, I heard a voice that commanded attention:

Ring of Power
Forged in the great elven tower
One of old
One foretold
May only bear
They, doth all evil fear
Savior of kings
Led by the One Ring

Suddenly I woke, sat straight up in my bed. There was a bright flash and it was daylight, but I was not in my bedroom or in my bed. I sat in the middle of a field and I heard the roar of voices in front and behind me. Then I saw about five hundred creatures rushing toward me. Some were on foot, others riding a whole array of creatures. There were several horses, a great lizard with wings that resembled a dragon, a lion with wings, an ostrich-looking thing, another creature that resembled a cross between a zebra and a bear, and several other animals I could not begin to describe.

The *people* were also of different sizes and descriptions. Some wore cloaks like a friar would, some looked like knights fully clad in armor. Others had robes and some were dressed like Vikings. They ranged in size from barely four feet tall to eighteen feet tall and every height in between. Most had a sword or some other weapon in one hand and a shield in the other. Some wore helmets, some did not. They all had one thing in common; there was hatred and bloodlust in their eyes.

When I turned around there was an almost identical array of creatures coming from behind. I saw dead and nearly dead bodies lying on the ground all around me as far as I could see in all directions.

There was another bright flash and I found myself in a large cave full of figures in hooded cloaks. They were all chanting in a language I could not understand. At the other end of the cave was a raised platform of solid rock. On this rock dais was a stone in the shape of a casket. A human figure that resembled a witch doctor danced around the stone *casket*. The chanting rose in volume and the crescendo increased rapidly. There was a small explosion and fire leapt to the ceiling from the *casket*. A figure sat up in it. At the same time, the chanting stopped and everyone, including the witch doctor, went down to their knees and bowed their heads to the floor. The figure in the coffin turned and stared straight at me. It had flaming red sockets where its eyes should be and a skeletal face you would only see in your worst nightmares. Its stare paralyzed me with fear. When it threw its head back and laughed with a horrendous bellow, my entire body shook.

Something grasped my arm; and when I turned to see what is was, I was back in the field again. There were creatures fighting all around me. I started to move and a half-decayed dead man held onto my left arm and muttered, "Help us!"

I woke up screaming in my own bedroom shaking and covered with sweat. I glanced at the clock, July 2, 10:00 a.m. I nearly jumped out of my skin when I heard someone knock on my front door. I pulled on my pants and shirt then headed for the door. Of course, Doc walked beside me as if he were leading the way. Before I reached the door, another knock sounded. Doc stopped in his tracks and growled. I took notice since it was the first time he had ever sounded a warning like that.

"What's the matter, Doc?' I opened the door and found a small man standing on my porch. He had a robe and hat on that looked like it came out of a theater prop room and he held a staff that was taller than he was. He had a boyish face that seemed out of place compared to his ancient eyes. He stood about five feet two inches tall and weighed roughly ninety pounds with long golden hair that looked almost like strands of silk that hung down to the small of his back.

"May I help you?' He paid no attention to me. Instead he stared off to my left side, presumably at Doc. "Don't worry, he won't bite." When I turned to my left I did not see Doc. My great protector was actually on my right sitting in the same spot he was in when I opened the door, but the stranger still looked to my left.

"Is there something I can do for you?' I put my left hand against the door frame as I leaned forward. When I did his gaze followed my hand and a smile crossed his lips.

"Yes. We need your help again."

His voice sounded musical, almost magical in a

way.

"How may I help you?"

"Our world needs you again."

"I think you have the wrong house."

"I don't think you understand."

"No, I don't. What do you want me to do?"

"I need you to come with me. We must hurry; there is no time."

"Where?"

"To Surrea, do you not remember? It has been a long time."

I wanted to let this crackpot down easy. "I'm sorry, but you have the wrong guy, please leave now. Good-bye." I shut the door before he could say anything else.

"I do not have the wrong one!"

It was the same voice, only more menacing. I swung around and stared at the same man in the middle of my living room standing behind Doc.

He pointed his staff at me and his voice no longer sounded musical. "You wear the Ring of Omens, you are the One!"

"How did you...?" I started to say as he waved his empty hand at me and then everything went dark.

CHAPTER TWO

Misery Loves Company

I woke to a large wet tongue licking my face. "Ok Doc, give me a sec." I opened my eyes and wondered how long I had slept since it was still dark. Then I realized I was not lying in my bed and was fully dressed.

I felt around because of the extreme darkness. I found myself sitting on a stone floor. I rubbed my eyes in the pitch black, but it did not help my sight. I groped around until my hands found a wall of the same material as the floor.

"Where in the hell are we?"

How would I know?

Which direction the voice in the darkness came from I could not tell; but it almost seemed to come from inside my head. "Who said that?" There was no answer. Maybe I was just dreaming. "Side Doc."

My voice did not sound very authoritative because fear had set in.

I'm already there, Barfsch.

"Who's there? Show yourself!" No one answered and I reached over and touched Doc. "Good boy." I patted his head and felt a little more secure with him there. I stood and reached for the wall again and used the stone to steady myself. It gave way. At first, I leaned against a solid surface and then found myself losing my balance and falling in the direction of the wall.

While I fell, I groped into the darkness and desperately looked for the wall that I knew had to be there. I found nothing, that is, until I landed on the floor. My right hand hit the rough stone and my left landed on something lying there. I also thought I noticed the ring I had placed on my left index finger glowing softly out the corner of my eye. Then it stopped glowing the moment I landed. I dismissed it thinking my eyes were playing tricks on me.

Are you alright, Barfsch? that strange voice said.

"No, I'm not." I answered, before I realized what I had done.

Did you hurt yourself, Barfsch?

"No, I didn't." *I just wish I knew where I was.* I picked up the item my hand fell onto.

I wish I could tell you, Barfsch, but I have no idea where we are either.

At first, it did not hit me, but suddenly I realized, I just thought the words, I did not speak them. I decided to experiment and forget about the object for now. *What is your name?*

You know as well as I do Barfsch, you named me.

Why don't you tell me anyway? The guy was evidently playing games with me, or I was going crazy, one of the two.

My name is Doc and yours is Barfsch.

I suppose that was to reassure me. Now I knew I was going crazy. *Dogs don't talk and they don't read minds, and my name is Tom, not Barfs.*

I have always talked, you just never listened and what do you mean by reading minds?

Ok Doc, if you understand me, lick my hand. I stuck my right hand out, the mysterious object still clutched in my left. My hand was being licked. It was Doc all right.

I can read your thoughts, huh? Well, when was the last time we went to sleep and woke up on a stone floor in the pitch-black darkness of a cave?

I put my thoughts toward the object I had found. It felt like metal, was very heavy, about three and a half feet long and flat with a razor-sharp edge on both sides. It came to a point on one end and had a hilt on the other. "A sword, I found a sword!" I grabbed the hilt and lifted it. Suddenly it felt light as a feather.

You have come back for me, my friend. It sure has been a long time.

The voice in the darkness was different. The metallic, magical tone reminded me of the little guy in my dream, or was I still dreaming? It all seemed so real.

You are not dreaming, this is reality, my friend.

"Who are you?" I inquired.

You do not remember? I am the Sword of Kar'itma, the Sword of Omens. The voice sounded triumphant.

"Great. A talking dog and a talking sword. What's next?"

A talking sword?

A talking dog?

Both voices questioned simultaneously.

"And I guess neither one of you can hear the other, right?" This situation got stranger by the minute.

Someone's coming. Doc said.

I looked up and saw a light a good distance from us that grew steadily closer. If there was one thing I knew in this absurd dream, I needed that light as much as I felt the urge to wake up.

"Come Doc." We headed toward the light cautiously, feeling the wall for guidance while I walked.

Doc growled. *And something else, Barfsch, I mean Tom, he's scared to death.*

Stop! The sword screamed. *There is a trap in front of you!*

My heart raced and I stopped. Since it was totally dark, I naturally could see nothing. *Where?*

In the middle of the floor, if you take another step, you will set it off!

Hold Doc, can we get around it, Sword?

Yes, have the dog follow behind you and stay against the wall on the left.

I quickly explained to Doc and we slid by the so-called trap. By this time, the light was close enough for me to see who held it. A little guy, about four feet three inches tall, scurried toward us as fast as his short legs could carry him.

He wore a light gray cloak like Friar Tuck in Robin Hood, he had a piece of rope for a belt with a long gray beard tucked underneath it. If his beard were not secured by his belt it might have dragged on the ground. He wore sandals, had a dagger stuck in his belt and carried a staff in his hand. There was a large book tucked under his arm that rubbed against the staff, and he held a torch in the other hand.

He ran closer and I thought how comical he looked, just like one of the dwarfs in Snow White, except for the look of despair on his ancient face. Then I heard a howling pack of dogs far behind him. When his light found us, he stopped dead in his tracks.

His eyes were wide with fear and his gaze darted around quickly as if he were looking for an escape route. He put the torch in his right hand along with the staff and book and drew his dagger with his left hand at a startling speed. His gaze fell upon me and it changed from fearful to menacing.

"Friend or foe?"

The man's voice was extremely deep for his size and sounded dangerous. "Friend. I am lost and…."

"There is not time."

He cut me off in mid-sentence and his tone turned from menacing to desperate.

"We must hurry, there are too many."

Ask him what is following him.

I did not hesitate to take the sword's advice. "What is following you?"

"Orcs, about twenty orcs."

When the little man ran past us, Sword reminded me about the trap. "Stop! There's a trap in front of you. Go along the wall on your right." I followed behind him and Doc followed me.

Stop here and fight... We will never outrun them and we can use the trap to our advantage.

From the sounds I heard the *orcs* were getting closer. I repeated what Sword said to the dwarf. Either he agreed or was just tired of running because he stopped and looked at me.

"I'm with you. Now's as good a time as any to die!"

"How encouraging." I shook my head, wanting to ask what an orc was, but there was no need. A weird-looking creature ran into the light. It was barely taller than the dwarf, with a hideous disfigured face and large yellow fangs protruding from a grotesque mouth. Yellow eyes with slits for pupils and long pointed ears did little to enhance the sickly green skin. It wore an animal hide for clothing and carried a wooden club in its four-fingered hand. The creature's arms and legs resembled an ape, and all of its exposed skin was covered with thick, coarse, brownish-orange hair.

When it came closer it let out a horrible cry, as if to signal the battle had begun. Three more orcs entered the light just behind the leader. They were replicas of the first one, except one carried a spear instead of a club which he threw at me. I jumped to the side and it harmlessly hit the stone floor behind me.

With the sword in hand and Doc behind me, we

skirted back along the wall and stood our ground behind the trap. All the ugly creatures rushed toward us. Then in one large flash they were gone. That was the last I saw of them. *What happened?*

Disintegrated. Sword stated. *Get ready now. The trap is no more...*

Two more orcs entered the light, then another. I noticed three more come into view just when the first two reached me. I thrust my blade into the mid-section of one and threw a roundhouse kick at the other's head. It connected and sent the orc flying into the wall. I watched it slide to the ground unconscious. The other one slumped to the floor dead.

"Two down, who's next!" My confidence rose higher so when the next one swung its club at me I parried the blow and brought my sword down on its head. There was a sickening crunch. Another one down.

Two more attacked from the right and a third on my left with a spear. I thrust at the one farthest right and kicked the one next to him in the throat. The first orc sidestepped my blow and swung at me; the second one dropped to his knees grabbing his throat. The third stabbed me in my left arm with his spear. I felt a searing pain but ignored it to block another blow from the one who woke up.

The one I kicked in the throat started to rise from his knees so I kicked him in the face and knocked him back in front of his companion who tripped over him and landed at my feet screaming loudly in pain. Then I put a sidekick into the face of the one on my right and felt his skull crack between my foot and the wall. I brought Sword down on the one on the floor when he started to get up and watched while that accursed spear came at my chest. It stopped mere inches before it hit me and fell to the floor. I glanced and watched the orc grab at the dagger that stuck out the side of his neck as he fell to the ground.

Thank God, that dwarf knew how to throw a knife! A moment later I slashed another orc across the chest when it ran up to me, club in hand. There were now eight bodies, dead or unconscious lying in front of me when four more orcs entered the light.

One had a spear, so I put Sword in my left hand and picked up the spear lying at my feet and threw it at the orc. The creature tried to sidestep my weapon, but he was not quick enough. The spear went into his chest and the point of it stuck out his back. "Ha, ha! Take that you slimy creature. Thirteen down, who's next?"

Watch out for the one with the sword, he'll be the leader and will know how to fight...

Sword had been right about everything, so I was not going to doubt it now. The one with the sword was bigger than any other orc I had seen yet. The *leader* yelled something I could not understand at the other two. It sounded like gibberish to me.

At first, they looked at me, and then they looked at their fallen comrades, then back at their leader. He yelled at them even louder and kicked the one nearest him and knocked him down. The other one hesitated and yelled while he charged me. I waited until the right moment, stepped to the side, grabbed

Sword like a bat and yelled, "Batter up!" I swung at his neck like a batter trying to hit a homerun.

"And it's a high fly ball!" The orc's head flew back toward his comrades, just as the other one got up. Seeing his friend's head hit the ground and roll up to him, he turned and ran. The leader yelled, stepped in front of him and cut him down.

"Now try me, human!"

The orc yelled at me with a deep-throated voice and charged. I stood ready. He swung his sword. I parried his attack and kicked at his head. He grabbed my foot with a speed I did not expect and threw me to the floor. He came at me fast, but I rolled away just as his sword hit the floor inches from my head. I kicked and caught him in the gut.

When he stumbled backwards, I rose to my feet. We walked in a circle and studied each other, both of us searching for a weak spot. Again, he swung.

Blocking his thrust and using a leg sweep, I caught him off guard and he went down. I took advantage of the situation and brought Sword down hard on his leg. When his bone cracked from the blow it echoed down the rock hallway. He howled then kicked me in the stomach.

I stumbled back and somehow, he managed to stand. I saw pain in his eyes. "Surrender or die!"

"I'll never surrender to human swirl!"

I picked up a spear from the ground beside me and walked toward him. "Then die!" I threw the spear hard and accurate. The moment it struck his chest he dropped his sword, grabbed at his chest where the spear entered, fell to the stone floor and took his last breath.

I leaned against the wall now that the battle was over and waited for my adrenaline *rush* to subside. Pain entered my consciousness. I was barely able to hold Sword with my left hand. I noticed my bright red blood running down my arm and mixing with the orc's green blood already covering my sword.

The dwarf ran here and there to check every body that lay on the floor. He held his dagger in one hand and a rope in the other. He stopped at one of the first orcs I fought, violently threw him over onto his stomach and proceeded to bind his hands and feet. While he did this, I heard a groan and saw an orc stir. I stepped on his head and put the point of my sword against the side of his bruised neck.

"I wouldn't move if I were you." And to impress the statement upon my adversary, I put a little pressure against my sword and watched the point dig in.

The dwarf slowly made his way toward me while Doc kept guard. Finally, he stood in front of me. "Check the others first." It was strange to hear that my voice had turned so hoarse. My ally nodded and walked off to do as I asked.

By the time he returned I felt faint. I relinquished my prisoner to him and managed to move closer to the wall to sit. My arm throbbed badly and I wished the pain would stop. My head swam and it was all I could do to remain conscious. The increasing pain in my arm kept me from blacking out.

The dwarf secured all the survivors, then came to my aid. He pulled a small black bag out of his cloak, and to my surprise he pulled out the book he was holding earlier. I thought my wound had made me incoherent, because the bag he held was much smaller than his book.

He opened the book and started to turn the pages. I could not comprehend what he was doing, so in my confused state I just stared. Here I was bleeding to death and he was reading a book! I hoped it was some kind of medical manual. He grabbed my good arm and put it to my side, then laid his hand over the wound.

"Un'tom inkto cranluss," he chanted, "lith'um iton'ito lustri!"

Upon stating the last word, his hand glowed with an eerie yellow light. I regained my senses and the pain suddenly disappeared. When he removed his hand, even my wound appeared completely healed with only a small scar.

The dwarf was amazing! "How did you do that?" He stared at me perplexed.

"A spell of healing, of course. You are a great warrior." He put the book back in his bag. "I've only seen one other fighter handle himself like that in all my days."

To my amazement, he pulled his four-foot staff out of the seven-inch black bag. I was totally bewildered. "What is your name?"

"Father Glumstron Stonefoot of the Silver Rock Clan, Disciple of Ich'banto Ironarm, at your service." He bowed. "And who might you be great warrior, who wears such unusual attire?"

"Tom Brown at your service." I tried to sound polite and tough at the same time.

"We must hurry, there's a chance we might be able to save my friends." There was an urgency to his request.

CHAPTER THREE

A Friend in Need Is A Friend Indeed

When I stood I did not expect the refreshed feeling that came over me. I felt as if I just had a good night's sleep. My new companion had such a long name I decided to just call him Glum. He started frisking the bodies, evidently looking for anything of value. I gathered up the three spears I thought might come in handy. Doc stood guard while we worked.

"Here."

Glum handed me eight coins and put four in his pocket.

"And I thought you might be able to use this." He held up a scabbard. "I got it off the big one."

I strapped the scabbard to my left side while Glum walked over and kicked one of the two live orcs in his gut. Then he spoke some kind of gibberish and kicked him again. The orc spit at Glum and mumbled some kind of reply. It must have been the wrong response because Glum bent over and slit the orc's throat. The other orc watched the ordeal and began to speak rapid gibberish when Glum approached him. Evidently, it was the right answer, because Glum's blade went to the orc's feet to cut the bindings instead of his throat. Glum picked the orc up by his hair and looked at me.

"Let's go."

I started to put Sword up, but it stopped me. *I can't communicate with you unless you hold me by the hilt. There could be more traps ahead.*

That sounded logical so I compromised. I sheathed Sword but kept my left hand on the hilt. I tucked two spears under my left arm and kept the third one in my right hand, ready for action.

We walked down the hallway, Glum in front holding the orc by his hair in front of him, his dagger pressed tightly against its throat. Doc and I remained in the rear. "What did you say to the orc back there?"

"Don't speak orcian, huh, Tom Brown? I told him to take us to his camp and quizzed him about how many we would find there, but of course I did not expect him to comply. This one," Glum shook his captive violently, "saw what happened to his friend and said he would be more than happy to submit. Didn't you, you buntling mold?" He laughed.

I listened while Glum talked with the captive. They talked their gibberish, but I still listened intently, even though it was the strangest language I had ever heard.

"He says there's twenty-six more of his friends left and three guard wolves."

I wondered what a *buntling mold* was but decided not to ask. "Where's their camp?"

"Well Tom Brown, this place is kind of a maze and even if our friend here was smart enough to tell us where his camp is, odds are we'd still get lost trying to find it. So, we'll just have to trust him to lead us to it."

I nodded and followed Glum and the captive from rooms and hallways to more rooms and hallways. We marched on making turns here and there. The place really was a maze. While we trudged along Glum told me how the orcs ambushed him and five of his friends. Glum became separated from his companions during the fight but saw one of his comrades killed and four captured. One was badly wounded and probably dead by now. I felt sorry for Glum. He seemed to have a bad case of survivor's guilt because he managed to escape.

"The orcs kill prisoners that are weak and make slaves out of the ones that survive. That means there's still a good chance three of them are still alive."

Doc stopped. *I heard something, and there's a strange odor in the air.*

"Glumstron."

"I heard him," Glum replied.

"Which way Doc?"

In front of us, whatever they are, they're moving this way.

Glum slowly backed up. Doc and I moved in

front of him.

"Give me your torch, Glum."

"I'll have to light it, hang on."

I turned and realized he was not carrying a torch nor had he had one for quite some time, yet, we were surrounded by light. Another curious thing I decided not to ask about.

"I've got a better idea instead, bring your spear here and watch our friend. If he gets away, not only will we not find my friends, but I doubt if we could find our own way out of here for quite some time." He took his book out of the black bag.

"How close are they, Doc?"

They stopped up ahead.

Glum thumbed through his book. "Let us know if they come this way,"

My stomach growled loudly and I wondered if he had any food.

Doc whined. *Ask him, I'm hungry too.*

I knew his black bag produced many things, but it did not seem big enough to hold meals for everyone. But I asked anyway, "you wouldn't have any food in that bag, would you?"

"No, but food can be arranged."

Who was I to question him? If we were hungry and he could feed us, more power to him. He was an increasingly interesting and astounding companion.

"Ah, here it is. Give me the tip of your spear." Glum reached toward me. "Alto'imbo recti'on tin ricti'finto clanitbonto asoon'il. Okay, now for some food."

Glum released my spear and started thumbing

through his book again. Did he have a secret compartment in there? He reached into his bag and pulled out a large cloth and spread it out on the ground. Reading from his book again, he recited another chant. After he said the last word, there was a flash of blue light and a platter with a roasted turkey, or at least it looked like a turkey, appeared out of nowhere on the cloth.

Once again, I decided not to ask. I was beginning to expect the unexpected in this wondrous place, wherever it was. I pulled off a leg and gave it to Doc, then dug in myself. We were all obviously famished and the wonderful aroma that filled the air made us want more. We merrily ate our feast and filled our bellies.

Doc stood. *They smelled the food and are coming this way. They're some kind of animal and there are three of them.*

Glum looked into the darkness. "Leave that spear here and let's move back. Maybe they are after the food and we will be able to see what they are. There are animals down here I would not care to run into."

Doing what he suggested, we waited at a safe distance away while the area around the food remained lit. A couple of seconds later, a very large grizzly bear cautiously entered the light. It slowly moved toward what was left of our meal. Two more grizzlies came into view and lumbered over to the carcass.

"I don't think we want to mess with these beasts," Glum whispered. "A couple of torches might not be a bad idea." He pulled out his black bag.

"Doc, see if you can communicate with them."

Doc tilted his head one way, then the other. *Not only can I talk with them, but I think I can control them.*

"Try."

What should I make them do?

"Have them lay on their backs."

We all watched in amazement while the three bears laid down and rolled onto their backs.

I not only have complete control over them, I can see what they see and hear what they hear. It's a new experience for me.

Doc was really excited and I could plainly see he was enjoying his newfound powers.

Glum stared at the grizzlies. "Ask them if they have seen our orcian friends."

No, they haven't.

"Well, we can use them to rescue my friends. But if we don't hurry there might not be anybody to rescue."

"Can you hurry them up?" I was thinking this would be one strange alliance.

Glum pushed his prisoner forward. The orc was reluctant to head toward the grizzlies. I cannot say I blame him since we were all a bit skeptical, but there was no time for doubt. "Doc, lead the way."

Ok Tom.

The grizzlies turned without finishing their meal and lumbered down the hall, which showed how much control Doc had over them. Doc fell into the routine of having the orc relay the directions and he in turn told the bears. It seemed Doc's telepathic ability broke down all language barriers. I told this to Glum and we decided to gag the orc, since Doc could communicate with him telepathically. That way in case the orc got brave and decided he wanted to be a hero and warn his comrades, he couldn't. We did not want to ruin our surprise advantage or take any chances.

Doc stopped, his tail straight out. *He says his camp is around the next turn. On the other side of a door, there is a large room and they're inside.*

Glum looked at Doc and whispered, "Ask him if there's another way into the room."

There's a door on the other side.

"Have the bears enter from that door. Think you can do that?"

I'll try.

The bears wandered by oblivious to us being there. I was beginning to appreciate Glum's strategic mind. After ten long minutes, Doc announced the bears' arrival at the door. It was closed. He also said he could hear noises inside through the bears. We bound the orc's feet so he could not wander off. Glum and I walked to the door and waited. Then the wolves inside began to bark.

"They caught the scent of the bears." Glum groaned. "Dog, have the bears attack. Send the bears to protect my friends. Let us know when they are inside and in position. Are you ready Tom Brown? Now is as good a time as any to die."

"That's not very encouraging. How about saying, now is not the time to die, but the time to kill them before they kill us." Glum looked at me with a strange expression on his face. "Well, it is more positive. l try to think positive."

They're in place, six orcs and one wolf, dead or wounded, and one bear is down. The other two are badly hurt.

We flung the door open and I yelled our arrival. I jabbed a knife into the back of the orc who guarded the door and he fell to the floor without a sound.

"That will teach you to take your attention away from your job." I threw my spear at the next one who managed to dodge my attack. Amazingly, my spear hit the orc behind him in the throat and he went down. I quickly threw my two other spears. One hit an orc, the other hit the wall and fell to the floor. Two out of three isn't bad I decided. Then I drew Sword and yelled again, which did seem to scare them. I charged the orc I threw the first spear at and met him halfway. Without trying, I parried his blow and crushed his skull.

The orcs were disorganized and confused. Then the largest one yelled at the others. This one had to be the leader.

Chieftain of his clan. Be very careful of him, he will be the deadliest. Sword stated.

Evidently, the *chief* told the others to ignore the bears and attack us. This was fortunate for us, because when the ones closest to the bears turned around and started to head my way, the two within striking distance of the grizzlies went down with their heads half torn off. I now had at least ten orcs heading straight for me. I killed the one immediately in front of me, then turned and ran back toward the door where Doc and Glum stood. I knew if I got surrounded, I would be in serious trouble. A spear flew by my head when I reached the doorway.

All three bears are gone, Glum's friends are free and I have control of the last wolf.

"Into the hall!" I commanded as I turned to face the onslaught. One orc came at me yelling with a club raised over his head ready to strike. That was a mistake. I leapt forward and gave him a front kick to the face which stopped him dead in his tracks. A quick easy jab to the chest and he was down. Two more rushed me. I slashed the first one across the chest, while moving to put that orc between me and the other one. This was nearly a fatal mistake, because I was cut off from the door. The one I had maneuvered away from was now between the door and me with several more closing in.

I had to act fast. If I did not get past that orc and get into the doorway immediately, I was dead. I rushed him as three more orcs came at my back. Before I could engage him, he fell over and I saw Glum's dagger in the center of his back. I finally reached the door and turned again.

That was the second time Glum pulled me out of a tight spot. When I turned there were four orcs heading my way, the rest were fighting Glum's friends. It appeared only eight orcs were still standing. I eased away from the door so only two could come through at a time.

Another orc came at me with a club raised over his head. I used the same technique that worked so well on the last one. Front kick, jab and he went down. Now there was a body partially blocking the door, so only one could come through at a time.

The next one had a sword and a shield. I already learned the hard way the ones with better weapons were better fighters, and I was not going to make the same mistake twice. Since he had a shield, I decided to let him have the first blow. I waited for the sword to make its swing, but instead he battered into me with his shield. Not expecting this, he caught me off guard. At the last second, I realized what he was doing and braced myself as best I could.

The ugly beast knocked me into the wall and I nearly lost my wind. Then his sword came down and I barely dodged the swing. This gave me the opportunity to use a leg sweep and he went down as I stabbed straight down into his chest before he could recover. He shivered a moment then went limp.

I had to duck a swipe by one of the two remaining orcs while I pulled Sword free of the still body. It barely missed me, the air from the swing brushing my hair. I crouched down, then brought my foot up and struck his groin with all my might. The blow picked the orc up off the ground by nearly two feet. His eyes rolled up into his head and he fell unconscious to the floor.

I blocked the last creature's blow, spun and brought Sword down between his neck and shoulder. The blade buried deep into his body. When he fell Sword was nearly yanked out of my hand. I had to plant a foot into the dead orc's mid-section and wiggle Sword back and forth until I could free it. I was lucky no more attacks came at me or I would have been weaponless.

I worked Sword's blade free and grabbed the shield the orc had. I ran back into the room just in time to see the chieftain shove his sword through the chest of the last of my allies. The chief was the only one left now and he eyed me carefully.

"I've already killed twenty of your slime ball followers. One more scum lord to kill is no problem. Go ahead, make my day. An orc chieftain hide will make a nice addition to my trophy room." Then I gave him my best smirk. I was not sure if I shook his confidence, but it sure did make him mad. Hopefully he would make a mistake.

He came at me like a wild bull. I blocked his blow and shoved into him with my shield. Since he was an experienced fighter he went with my *push*. He grabbed my shield and flung me past him. I fell flat on my face. I stumbled and quickly recovered, but not quickly enough. The very tip of his sword slashed me across the back. The cut was not deep, but it was enough to make me nearly drop Sword. I turned when he swung again and blocked his blow with my shield. His sword cut through it like it was made out of tinfoil. I kicked him as hard as I could in the groin and blocked his next stroke with Sword. My kick seemed to have no effect on him and I got a fist across my lip for the effort. I stumbled back and barely managed to block the next blow.

Either this guy was a machine, or he was on drugs. I countered with a thrust, which he deflected and managed to hit me in the face again with his fist. I tasted blood in my mouth and decided I needed a better strategy since he was beating the hell out of me. I waited for his next attack which I blocked. I kicked him in the nose with a spinning heel kick and he stumbled back. Then I used a roundhouse kick to the ear that dazed him and I knew I had to strike. I thrust with all my might, straight at his chest and connected. He went to his knees, but still managed to swing one last time.

I let go of Sword and jumped back, barely getting out of the way as the tip of his sword slashed through my shirt without touching me. To my surprise, he got back on his feet and slowly stumbled toward me. Green blood dripped down his chin from the corner of his mouth. No more messing around. I picked up a spear lying on the ground and lunged toward him. The spear found its mark in his mid-section while he lumbered toward me. He stumbled back and fell lifeless to the ground. After a few twitches and one last gasp, I knew he was dead.

Glum and Doc came into the room and Glum went over to where his friends lay.

Glum sat on the ground beside his friend. "It's too bad he had Kern's Blade of Cutting."

This was not the time to ask what that meant so I walked over to the dead orc who still had Sword in him and retrieved my trusty weapon while Doc stood guard. I walked over to console Glum and found him down on his knees with his book open. I bent over and felt for a pulse on his friend; but there was none. I wondered what Glum was doing. Maybe he had prayers in his book.

While Glum thumbed through the pages I looked the room over and found an orc still breathing. I started to ask Glum if we wanted him alive, but when I turned to ask him I stared in bewilderment. My mouth hung open, but not a word came out.

Glum glowed like an angel, with bursts of bright white light flowing up and back down in an arc, that looked like sun flares. He had one hand on the chest of his dead friend, and the other above his head. He chanted with his book lying open at his side. After the last word of his chant the light flowed from him, through his hand and into the dead body lying in front of him. To my amazement, the corpse stirred. Glum collapsed and fell to the floor.

Doc barked. *Watch out behind you, Tom!*

I turned to see the orc I had found alive trying to stand. Still bewildered by the spectacle I just witnessed, I did not want to mess with the orc so I chopped him down before he could completely get up.

When I turned back around, I found myself staring into the eyes of someone who just rose from the dead and was now sitting up breathing. The hole in his chest looked like an old scar. He did seem dazed and bewildered.

I stepped closer to Glum to make sure he was all right. I abruptly turned back toward Glum's friend who apparently had snapped out of his daze. He grabbed a nearby club, jumped to his feet and challenged me.

"Friend or foe?"

Before I could answer I saw Glum staring at me with a rather odd look so I hesitated.

"Relax Glamrock." Glum held up his hand. "He helped me rescue you. If it wasn't for him and his talking wolf, you would have been an orcian slave, or worse."

"I warrior, Glamrock Clapstone of Tooth Clan, at your service, I ever be in your debt."

He sounded a like three-year-old learning to talk, but he was sincere and thankful for my help. "Tom Brown of the Earth Clan, at your service. You have no need to apologize, one cannot be too careful." I looked at Glum. "Will he be all right?"

"Who Glumstron? Be fine. You never see raising of dead be'fo?"

"No."

Now I had a Glum, a Glam, a Doc and Sword for companions." I took a deep breath. *The name Tom seems out of place here. Maybe I will change my name to something more suitable for a warrior.* I thought to myself.

How about Sterling? That was your name long ago.

I did not ask what it meant by *was*. How much could a talking sword know anyway? I went back to checking bodies.

Help Tom! Doc pleaded as I heard him barking in the hall. I ran to his aid and found an orc swinging a club at him. The orc saw me coming, turned and ran. I let him go.

He was trying to set the other one free, so I kept him busy until you could get here.

I petted Doc's head and gave him a hug. *Thanks buddy.* He really was a great companion and I was lucky to have him. But right now, I needed to finish checking the bodies. Glum was up now, gathering useable weapons and supplies. Glam guarded the other door. I made the rounds picking up weapons and coins. I found twenty coins, three spears and a sword. I cut the bonds on the orc's feet, gathered everything, then took him and the items I found into the room. I closed the door and told Doc to keep a watch on it. After I piled the items in the center of the room, I kicked the orc's feet out from under him. He fell flat on his back and I pointed a finger at him menacingly. I think he got the idea, because he never tried to get back up.

I looked over at Glum. "Are you going to bring your other friends back to life?"

"I don't have the power. Once you've been decapitated, that's it. Only an Arch Father or a wish has that kind of power.

When I looked at his other three companions I saw what he meant.

Glum shook his head. "Unfortunately, the chieftain used Kern's sword."

I wondered what Glum meant, but wisely decided not to ask.

CHAPTER FOUR

How Tall Did You Say It Was?

We made camp in the orcs' room. Both doors swung into it, so we put two bodies on the outside of each door and piled the rest against the closed doors on the inside. Glum had told me that if something was drawn to the dead bodies, it would hopefully be satisfied by the two outside. The rest should keep just about anything from getting into the room.

I wondered what he meant by; *just about anything*. Nothing short of a battering ram could budge fifteen bodies. Even as small as orcs were, I would say they weighed eighty to one hundred-eighty each, plus the bears, wolves and Glum's friends. Then again, I had never heard of a talking dog or sword, not to mention resurrecting the dead. I had a queer feeling I was in for many more surprises.

Glum whipped up another feast, this time it looked like a roast pig. There were also fruits and vegetables. He pulled a wine flask out of that bag of his and we chowed down. After we ate, Glum healed the wound across my back since it hurt and kept bleeding. His *healing spell* reminded me of an old ad on TV that said *stops the stinging on contact*.

Right now, I was a happy camper since my belly was full and the pain was gone. I bid everyone good night, went over and laid down against the wall. Glum came over and handed me seventy coins.

"You did most of the fighting, these are yours."

"My pockets are stuffed with coins already. I would trade all the coins I have for a nice soft bed right now."

"I don't have that." Glum laughed. "But I do have a couple of pelts you could sleep on."

"If it won't put you out."

"Put me out where?"

"It's a figure of speech. It means if it isn't inconvenient."

"Ah, but you do talk strangely. Both of us owe you our lives. According to law you own us and everything we own."

"Wow." I shook my head. "I release you from your debt to me. Besides, you saved my life twice today. But I would appreciate those pelts."

He pulled two pelts from his black bag and handed them to me. They made the stone floor a little more bearable. Doc came over and laid next to me. I edged over so he could share the comfort of the pelts since he more than deserved a little coddling. Glum and Glam were drinking wine and bragging about old battles, and that is all I remember before I drifted off to sleep.

I woke up in the middle of a meadow. An array of creatures ran by me as fast as they could. I grabbed the first human I saw. "What's going on?"

"Run, run for your life! Hide! Sar'garian is coming!"

The man screamed like a raving lunatic. He pulled free of my grip and ran as fast as he could. I shrugged my shoulders, laid down and fell back asleep.

Someone grabbed my arm and shook me. I opened my eyes and found Glum staring into them. "Wake up, we need to break camp and move on."

"Have you ever heard of a Sar'garian?" Glum's happy smile immediately turned so worried I thought he might turn and run.

"Shh! Do not even think that name. He has spies everywhere!"

The moment the words left Glum's mouth he quickly looked around the room as if he expected someone to magically appear. He sat down next to me and told me of an evil wizard that lived a thousand years ago.

"According to legend, he was very powerful and tried to take over The Great Southern Kingdom of Kal'ijora. The King, being very wise, tricked the wizard into coming to his castle alone. Being very over-confident he accepted and appeared without his forces. The King enlisted three very powerful magicians to kill the evil wizard. There was a long battle among the four. It is now called The Battle of

Four Mages. The evil wizard killed two of the three, before the third one finally killed him."

"The evil wizard was so powerful, he came back to life two hundred years later. He became one of the undead creatures' legends call a lich, the most powerful lich our world had ever seen. This undead creature had the dark forces at his disposal and went on a rampage like no living or dead being has ever seen. Kingdoms fell one after another to his massive armies.

"Four kingdoms were all that stood between him and total domination, Kal'ijora, Kar'itma, Kim'imota and Jar'lin. The kings of these great kingdoms got together and made a plan. They sent the most powerful magician among them, Asmond Hir'thito, to find the greatest warrior alive. He brought back a great warrior, Sterling the Great."

The name shocked me; it was the same one Sword called me.

"He was just in time. Kal'ijora was the only kingdom left. They gave the four great items to Sterling; the Sword of Kar'itma, the Shield of Jar'lin, the Armor of Kim'imota and the Ring of Kal'ijora."

Then I remembered that was the name Sword called itself. Then this was the sword of Sterling?

"He took the four great items of Omens and went to the battle ground."

I remembered the little guy in my dream the night before last called this ring I had, the Ring of Omens.

Glum continued. "Sterling appeared on the battlefield between what was left of the forces from the four Great Kingdoms of the South, and the lich's armies. He challenged the lich to battle, but the evil one was so sure of his power he deemed the puny warrior unworthy of his attention. Therefore, he sent his strongest warrior to accept the challenge. The two warriors fought for just seconds before Sterling stood victorious.

"Sterling once again challenged the lich and this time he accepted. Their fight lasted for several hours. The lich appeared to be besting Sterling when a great wolf appeared and distracted the lich just long enough to give Sterling the edge. He took his sword and finally slew the great evil.

"That was eight hundred years ago and the lich's followers have brought him back to life once again. He is the one *you* named. Legend has it that Sterling will return to battle him again, once and for all. That is why we are here." Glum pointed at Glam. "We were sent by Prince Al'sworth to find The Great Asmond Hir'thito. He was last known to reside here in Horzule's Keep. There were ten of us when we began, now there are only two of us. I am afraid we have failed, because we lost the Stone of Direction. Without it I doubt if we can ever find the great wizard. Now we will have to return in disgrace."

Poor Glum was so troubled he covered his face with his hands and fell silent. I then described the little guy in my dream to Glum. He immediately dropped his hands and lit up like a Christmas tree.

"That is Asmond! Where did you see him?"

Glum was very excited as I explained how I came across the ring, my dreams, how I stumbled onto Sword and then him.

"Let me see the ring."

Glum looked ready to jump up and down like a child wanting to open Christmas presents. I tried to take the ring off, but it would not budge. It would not even twist around on my finger. It was like it was glued in place, yet it had slid on so easy. Another thing in this place that did not make sense. "It won't budge." I held my hand out so Glum could see the ring. His eyes lit up and he looked at me in disbelief.

"It is the Ring of Omens!" Glum took a deep breath. "Now I know why Prince Al'sworth sent us here. It wasn't to find Asmond, it was to find you!"

"But I'm not this Sterling. I have always been Thomas Brown." I said it to convince him, but somehow, I felt like I was trying to convince myself.

"Humans only live a hundred or so years. Of course, you would not know, but the ring does. It found you, you didn't find it."

Glum said that with such authority I began to doubt my sanity. I knew who I was, or did I? I had to be dreaming, but it was all so real. Could I be this Sterling character reincarnated? I did not ask for this, I was perfectly happy back on earth, wherever that was. Why did the ring pick me? I was confused. There was a struggle going on inside me and I was losing touch with reality. "Who am I?" I screamed that question as loud as I could even though Glum was right in front of me.

Settle down Tom.

Doc's voice soothed my crazy thoughts. Doc managed to bring me back to whatever reality I was currently experiencing. At least my dog knew who I was. Now, what did Asmond call this world? Ah yes, Surrea.

"The first thing we need to do is find the other two items of Omens. Then if you're not Sterling, maybe Asmond will find him and we can deliver them to him." Glum was obviously trying to calm me down. "I'm hungry, how about you? Yes. I shall conjure a meal."

I watched him wave his arms and listened while he chanted something. Breakfast appeared and we all dug in and ate our fill. We then began to collect everything we needed for our venture. Glum put the extra weapons, and all the coins we found in his *magic bag*.

"How much will that hold?" That bag totally amazed me.

Glum smiled. "I don't know. I have never filled it up."

Since there were only two and a half shields, Glum told me to take one. He gave the other one to Glam and kept the half shield for himself. I carried a spear in my right hand, had the shield on my left arm while grasping Sword's hilt in its sheath. I noticed Glum had put a sword in his bag. I asked why he did not use it and he said it was against his religion to use a sharp weapon, except for his ceremonial dagger.

Glum explained how he carries a mace in his bag, but gave up using it because he was such a lousy fighter. He then told me about the last time he got into a hand-to-hand fight, one of his companions almost got his head cut off trying to come to his aid when the fight went against him. Luckily, his friend only got killed and after Glum brought him back to life he swore never to get into hand-to-hand combat again, unless there was no other possible option.

I still was not used to hearing things like, *he only got killed* and *brought back to life*. "Is there a limit to raising the dead?"

"With each person it is different, some can be brought back a couple of times, others seem to have no limit. There are times the spell does not work. It all depends on the individual's stamina and injuries."

He looked at me and his eyes narrowed. "Legend has it that Sterling was not of this world either." That last statement came out of nowhere and took me by surprise. The man was a wealth of information about this land I knew nothing about. I was eager to learn all its secrets, but now was not the time.

We then pulled the bodies away from the door and made our exit. After a short distance the orc told us the stairway to the next level was nearby, so we headed there. Doc and I led with Glum and our captive in the middle, while Glam brought up the rear. The more I saw of this place, the more I felt like a mouse in a maze. We went by countless passages that led somewhere else. We made many turns, took many passages, passed several rooms that looked just like ones we passed before. Just when I began to think the orc had led us astray, we came to a stone staircase that spiraled upward.

"This is it," Glum said. "It leads up to the next

level."

We climbed the winding stone steps to the top and found ourselves in a very large well-lit room that was roughly eighty feet wide by one hundred and sixty feet long and fifty feet tall. It had a large hall at the other end that was partially engulfed in darkness. I couldn't see any other exits from this room and for some reason that made me uneasy. When we were about halfway across the room, Doc stopped but remained in a very attentive stance.

I sense two human minds in the hall in front of us. Not very bright though.

Then a boulder the diameter of my waist flew at us from the darkness. "Stone Giants," Glum yelled. "Split up!"

The rock barely missed Glam, as another one flew straight at me. I tried to duck, but there was no time. I braced my shield between the huge rock and myself. It hit my shield like a battering ram. I flew backwards and my shield was ripped from my arm and sent through the air. I have no idea where it landed but I heard the metal hit the flat rock floor. My left arm was numb. I tried to move it, but nothing happened. I had to drop my spear to get up. When I reached my knees, another rock flew at me and I dropped back to the floor. I laid flat just in time for the rock to buzz over me.

The feeling in my arm began to return and now I wished it had stayed numb. It hurt like hell. I still could not move it and decided it must be broken. I slowly rose to my feet, cautious of more rocks that might have my name on it. None came. I reached for my spear on the floor and nearly passed out from the pain in my left arm and shoulder. I managed to pick it up fighting the darkness that tried to consume me.

At first, I thought I was staring at a hallucination. When Glum mentioned giants, I imagined them to be around eight to ten feet tall. Instead I saw an eighteen-foot monster step into the lighted area at the head of the hall.

This creature carried a stone club at least seven feet long and wore pelts for clothing. If the situation was not so serious, I would have laughed at how much Glam and the giant looked alike. They both wore pelts in the same fashion and both had the same stern, hard-looking features. The only differences were the weapons and shoes, Glam held a shield and sword and was wearing lace-up leather boots. The giant was barefoot and only carried a club. Even more surprising, the second giant was a good two-feet taller than the first, but other than that they were identical.

Even though my arm hurt beyond belief, I had no choice but to stand and fight. For every one of his steps, I would have to take at least three, so there was no way to outrun them. Glam, who was not touched by the barrage of rocks, stood ready to fight the one coming at him, but Glum and Doc were nowhere to be found. I focused on the giant running straight at me.

CHAPTER FIVE

Which Way Is South?

I threw my spear and it found its mark in the giant's left hip. The giant let out a howl that sounded like it came from a megaphone stuck in my ear. He grabbed the spear that looked like a toothpick in his massive hand and pulled it out. He snapped it like a twig and threw it down. The anger in his stern features deepened the closer he came. At least he now had a slight limp.

I wished I had the other spears that were still in Glum's bag and knew where my shield had gone. Even if I had my shield I doubt it would do any good. If he hit me with that huge club, it would compare to being in a Volkswagen Beetle instead of a motorcycle when a semi hit you. At least I still had Sword so I pulled it out and stood at the ready while the giant approached.

Good, a Stone Giant. This ought to be fun!

Fun? You must be kidding. You're not the one that is going to get squashed by that club.

Wait for him to swing, then dodge and go for the leg, I'll do the rest.

I hope you know what you're doing. Nobody I knew would believe I was talking to a sword in the midst of a battle. Hell, I barely believed it. The giant converged on me and swung his club in an arc. I leapt backwards as fast as I could to miss his swipe. I felt the wind from his massive club while I fell flat on my back. I started to get up and pushed with my arm, but the sharp pain reminded me it was broken. I had almost made it to my feet when the giant swung straight down. I rolled away a second before his club hit the ground. I reached out and swung for his leg. Considering the length of Sword, my swing would have brought me no closer than a foot away from the giant's leg. However, when my swing came around, Sword's length increased and hit the giant. It seemed to go through his leg like warm butter. The giant let out a yell twice as loud as before. He toppled, dropped his club and grabbed for the foot that was no longer there. I had completely severed his leg just above the ankle.

Jumping up, I thrust Sword into the giants' side and watched as the beast took its last breath.

I turned to see how Glam was doing. Unfortunately, not very well. I looked just in time to see him take a hard hit. The giant's swing reminded me of a golf pro making a long drive. I expected him to yell *fore* when Glam flew through the air.

There were three spears lying on the ground that

I had no idea where they had come from, so I picked one up and let it fly. The giant had his back to me, his club raised above his head ready to deal the final blow to Glam. My spear hit him in the kidney and the giant let out an anguished cry. He dropped his club and grabbed for the spear. Picking up another spear as the giant turned toward me, I buried it in his gut. He doubled over in sheer agony. I picked up the last spear by my feet and threw a lucky shot. The spear went straight into the front of his mouth and stuck out the back of his throat. He fell to his knees choking. As crushed as Glam was, he managed to thrust his sword into the giant's side. The giant fell flat on the floor and spit up more blood than I had ever seen.

I went over to Glam and pulled him away from the dying giant. Glum, the orc and Doc emerged from inside the stairway. Glum went over to see to Glam's wounds. I waited for the giant to quit breathing, then checked the bags each had tied to their sides. I found three hundred and four coins, a shield and a ring. I then pulled out the three spears I used to kill them, but one broke. By the time I was finished, Glam was back to his old self again and I got a big smile from Glum when I showed him the items I found. Glum was more than happy to store the coins away.

Glum pulled out his book and began to chant. Soon two of the items he had laid on the ground began to glow with an eerie reddish light.

"They're magical all right." Glum looked up. "Here Tom Brown, take the shield since you're the one keeping us alive. Glamrock can have the ring and I'll take your shield."

I traded him shields and he put the extra spear back in his black bag. He then healed my arm, along with my other cuts and bruises and we continued on our way.

The orc led us through a *secret* exit to the next stairway and we continued without any complications. The stairs went up twice as far as the last ones did and abruptly ended at a stone wall. Glum relinquished his prisoner to me then began to search the wall. I watched intently while he grabbed one stone after another until he finally found a stone that moved. He slowly pushed it into the wall and the wall opened inward like a door.

"I think this is level six or seven. I'm not sure."

Glum's voice was filled with an unmistakable disdain. I decided this was not the time to question him.

Once again, we continued on to the next stairway and climbed to its peak without problems. We emerged into a room that looked just like the room on the last level, and the level before that one. So far, other than giants, we had not seen a living thing or come across any *traps*. I always became suspicious when things went too well.

The orc says there's something he calls a teleport trap up ahead that goes to the second level.

'That means we'll be out of here in no time," was Glum's reply to the news. We all headed straight to where the orc said the trap would be. When Doc and I stepped into the area of the trap there was a blinding flash of orange light that consumed us.

I was no longer in the hallway where I had just been, I now found myself standing in a room alone. Luckily, I was still enveloped by the same light we had been seeing by since I met Glum, I had no idea how, but was very thankful I was. I walked to the only door and opened it. I hoped to figure out where I was, even if every room, hall and door looked the same. There were no landmarks, but I heard something in the darkness that loomed in front of me.

It was a dog barking in the distance. I hoped it was Doc. I started out at a fast jog, but when I heard the dog yelp in pain I broke into a full run. *I'm coming Doc!* When I turned a corner Doc's voice entered my mind.

Help Tom! There are too many for me to control.

I went another ten steps. Doc entered my light at a full out run chased by giant rats just barely smaller than him. I threw my spear at the closest one. I nearly made another fatal mistake, and this time Glum was not here to pull me out of the fire. My spear missed its mark, and when it skidded down the hallway, the light that had encircled me followed the spear and I now realized the *spell* Glum had put on it when he touched it. I dared not think what would have happened if that spear would have buried itself into the giant rat.

I felt Doc rush by me, since I was now engulfed by total darkness and could no longer see him or the lead rat. I jumped forward as far as I could to clear the rodent. Once over the monstrous beast I drew my sword. *You're going to have to handle him yourself, Doc.* I attacked the next one in line before it entered the darkness.

Sword came down on the rodent and it expired with a loud squeal. I edged forward swinging Sword back and forth, slicing first one then another. Over and over I repeated this process, until there was a pile of withering corpses scattered around me. I must have killed at least thirty of the filthy creatures by the time I reached the spear lying on the ground. I was tired and wondered how many more of these nasties there were.

Doc growled. *Several hundred. There's something coming behind us.*

I hope the thing behind us is a giant tom cat.

It's Glumstron and Glamrock.

Tell them to hurry! My arm was beginning to cramp, I had no choice but to fight on. After I killed about forty more of them, a bag flew over my head. It hit the ground and burst, spreading an oily substance everywhere in front of me.

I cut down two more when Glam warned me he was coming up on my left side. I moved to the right and slashed another creature. Glam maneuvered in beside me with a torch in his hand. He promptly threw the fiery end into the center of the non-stop horde that pushed toward us, their teeth dripping with saliva in anticipation of a bite of our flesh. The torch hit the ground and the hallway in front of us became a blazing inferno. I killed the last three rats that were on our side of the blaze.

Glum grabbed my shoulder. "Let's go. The fire will only hold them back a few minutes."

I picked up my spear and hurried out of the area while Glam and Glum led the way. Doc and I brought up the rear in case the giant rats followed us. We marched for fifteen minutes before I realized the orc was missing. "Where's our prisoner?"

"He tricked us." Glum lowered his head. "The trap was evidently an individual teleport that randomly sent us to different locations in the complex. Luckily it must have been set to this level since we all ended up on it." Glum looked up. "It's still possible we could bump into the lying ogre dung."

I nodded and we all continued on our way, to where I was not sure. After two hours of roaming the hallways we finally came upon another stairway that led up. We climbed it and came out into a room just like the one at the end of the first stairway we had climbed.

At first, I thought we might be back where we started, except the room had three doors that led out. Glum headed for the door on his right without hesitation, like he knew exactly where he was.

After twenty minutes of traveling in what seemed like circles to me, we came to an enormous door twice as large as the biggest one I had seen yet. It spanned a hundred feet and was at least eighty feet tall. I doubt even one of those giants could have budged it. Glam walked over to the handle. To my surprise, the door swung open easily with a long, loud creak.

We walked outside into an alcove. I was completely blinded by the sunlight that streamed into our little world. It took a couple of minutes for my eyes to adjust. I walked out of the alcove and looked upon a wondrous scene. There were two suns and one moon in the sky over Surrea. We were at the base of a lone mountain that looked like a volcano in the middle of a soft rolling, grassy field.

The flowers and plants were alive with the most vivid colors I had ever seen. I felt like I just stepped into the Land of Oz. The view was breathtaking. In the near distance, there was a herd of creatures that resembled bison, except they each had a tail more like a lion, with quills like a porcupine at the tip of it. They were bright orange with purple stripes that resembled a zebra's. As strange as they appeared, they seemed to belong in this alien landscape.

"Where go we?" Glam asked.

Glum stuck out his chest and took a deep breath. "I guess we better head back to Kal'ijora."

I looked in all directions. "Which way is that?"

Glum pointed in the direction I had indicated. "Straight north."

The next thing I knew I pointed in the opposite direction. "We need to go south, immediately." Glum stared at the hand I pointed with, and when I looked at the Ring of Omens, I noticed it was glowing softly. So that was where my statement originated.

"South it is." Glum stated his agreement without a bit of hesitation and he took off in the direction I pointed. We traveled for days. The countryside changed from fields to flat plains, then rolling hills sparsely covered with trees. Every once in a while, we would come across a herd of creatures; some looked like antelope, others looked like a cross between an ape and giraffe.

However, the strangest critter looked like a huge

brain with four stout legs and long antennas with eyes at the ends. This was the only beast we had seen roaming around by itself, and so far, the only one Glum purposely tried to avoid. He called it a Brainton, saying it was very hard to kill and very dangerous.

We had traveled for eight days avoiding any confrontations with the few hostile creatures we had seen. We came to a gigantic forest with trees bigger than the redwoods in California back on good old mother earth. The whole time I had not seen a sign of any kind of civilization.

"The Tar'loon Forest, we dare not enter it." Glum sat on the ground. "Those who enter do not live to tell their tale."

"The item I seek is in the center of these woods."

I now hated the ring stuck on my finger. I did not appreciate it taking control of my thoughts. This was the second time I had seen fear in Glum's eyes. He kept shaking his head, but he finally rose to his feet and marched into the forest. It was clear that Glum had the determination to succeed on our quest no matter the cost.

As soon as we were deep into Tar'loon, the wind that had been blowing died down and everything became eerily still. It had become dark enough we needed a light to see where we were going even though it was the middle of the day. I had a queer, uneasy feeling that we were being watched.

We trudged on the rest of that day. It seemed like the brush in front of us was too thick to penetrate, but by the time we got to it, there was always a sparse enough patch to get through. After hours of seeing this *illusion* over and over, I felt the forest was leading us to where it wanted us to go. We were going in the direction I sensed we needed to, so I did not mention my observation to the others.

We came to a small clearing, and since it was getting dark enough to hinder our journey we decided to make camp. Glum would not let us have a fire, so we sat huddled together in the darkness. No one said a word the whole night; it was as if we were afraid of attracting something to our presence.

Every once in a while, I would hear a twig snap close by, or a crash in the distance, as if one of the colossal trees suddenly uprooted and crashed down. Doc curled up beside me and put his head on my lap. He slept like a baby. I stroked his fur and knew I had my old friend back. Doc comforted me, but I still had a hard time sleeping in this strange, gloomy place.

I woke up like I did every morning in Surrea, thinking I just had the weirdest dream ever, only to find myself still in it. This was the last time I felt this might be a dream.

Everyone else was up and Glum had already conjured up breakfast. I ate quickly and Glum sensed my impatience to move on.

Glum warned the longer we sat in one place the better the chance something would find us so it was better to keep moving in Tar'loon. Considering the creatures I had seen so far and how nervous Tar'loon made Glum, I was in no hurry to find out what the *something* he referred to might be.

We quickly picked up camp and moved further into the darkness of Tar'loon. We traveled for four days, each one being just like the day before, until we had our first encounter with one of Tar'loon's inhabitants.

CHAPTER SIX

The Tree of Many Names

We marched in single file, Doc and I in front, then Glum, and Glam. It seemed like a never-ending trek, and with that thought Doc froze.

Something is close by.

"Which direction?" Glum asked.

Can't tell, but he's very close, and extremely intelligent.

Glum nodded. "Let's go quickly!"

We ran down the path in front of us until it abruptly disappeared and thick impassable tundra took its place. "Backtrack!" When I turned around I found a tree standing exactly where we had just stood. It was only twelve feet high to its top branches with a four-foot thick base. It had four knots that looked like a face and to my astonishment, the knot that looked like a mouth opened and began to speak.

"What are you doing in my forest?"

I found the tree's deep resonating voice very intimidating.

"Oh, noble Tre'ton, we have come because of a noble quest. My companions and I are here to find an item of Omens." Glum bowed at the waist. "The evil of the elder Tre'ton legends walks the plane of the prime material again. I travel with the savior himself. It is once again time for all good to reunite. I, Father Glumstron Stonefoot of the Silver Rock Clan, Disciple of Ich'banto Ironarm, have spoken the truth or may my arms wither and my legs rot."

"If what you say be the truth, noble dwarf, I will do all that is in my power to aid your noble quest. I, Stumlink Nosred'neh Trebor, of the Golden Breeze Clan, have spoken the truth or may my leaves never feel the sunlight again." The tree roared triumphantly.

"I need to find the Tree of Many Names." I was starting to get used to the ring taking control of me, but I still did not like it.

"Who is this impertinent sapling, noble dwarf, who dares to address an elder Tre'ton in such an insolent manner?"

"Noble Stumlink Nosred'neh Trebor, forgive his insolence, for he is the redeemer."

"Forgive me noble warrior, I was not aware that you are the One. I know now you are not familiar with elder Tre'ton customs. I apologize and will not make this mistake again. I, Stumlink Nosred'neh Trebor of the Golden Breeze Clan, have spoken the truth or may my bark be infested with bormites. If it is the Tree of Many Names you seek, I will gladly take your noble party there. But first, let me provide the hospitality of an elder Tre'ton, before we start such a long and dangerous journey."

"Your kindness is gladly accepted, Noble Tre'ton." Glum bowed.

When all the formalities were finished, the Tre'ton walked on its roots and we followed the massive creature's lead. We walked for half an hour and came to a large clearing with a gigantic tree in the center. The Tre'ton lumbered up to its base and waved one of his branches. A large opening magically appeared and the Tre'ton disappeared into its confines.

He beckoned us to follow so we did without hesitation. Once all of us were inside, the opening disappeared. Once again, I was totally amazed. The dimensions inside were twice as large as the outside of the extremely huge tree. There was a small stream running through it on one side and an array of vegetation growing everywhere. The Tre'ton strolled over to a stump in the middle of this wondrous domain and perched on it.

"Make yourself at home, noble sires."

Waving one of his branches as he said this, three stumps and a patch of grass rose from the ground and we all picked a stump to sit on while Doc laid down on the soft grass. I watched Glum reach over and pick a multi-colored mushroom and pop it into his mouth. I copied his example, not wanting to insult the Tre'ton again. The mushroom had the texture of cooked meat and tasted like a green apple. As I savored the food, the Tre'ton began to speak.

"We are the eldest race on Surrea. I am two thousand, one hundred and twenty-three years old. I am one of the few mortal beings left that was present at the last Great War between Good and Evil. I witnessed the destruction of the Great Evil first hand and attended the Circle of Legends when it was foretold that the Great Evil would come again. The Teller of Legends foretold of the Savior's return and the destruction of the Great Evil once and for all. However, I must warn you; he also saw a fault in the prophecy. The powers of evil forced its presence into the realm of space and time, trying to alter fate to its own desire, thus causing a rift of uncertainty."

"The Teller of Legends saw the possible destruction of all that is good. It is all up to *The Chosen One* now; only he has the power to destroy the Great Evil that cannot be called by its name. The fates have been tampered with. Our existence is unknown. The scales of chance have been put into motion. The outcome is undecided. The time has come for rest; our journey begins on the morrow."

With that last statement he waved a limb and three beds of straw and leaves emerged from the ground. We laid on our respective beds, exhausted from our strange journey. I closed my eyes and contemplated the words I just heard.

I floated above an encampment and assessed what lay below. Several creatures stood around a five foot round black disc held in the air by an unseen force four feet off the ground. A map of sorts lit up inside its confines that would change at times. A hooded, commanding figure spoke battle orders to his troops.

"We have succeeded in crushing the puny resistance of the North and Eastern sticktles. I want the head of King Nayr Derf within one moon, or I will have yours!"

The voice echoed as if it were not real, yet it was extremely forceful and evil.

"But Sire, there is strong resistance. It may…."

Before the beast could finish his statement, the hooded figure pointed a hand at him that looked more like a skeleton's hand than a living flesh and blood creature. A blue beam of light came out of the eerie hand and struck the creature who vanished with a scream of excruciating agony.

"Are there any more excuses?"

"No sire!" The other creatures responded as one.

"Now go and be victorious!"

After saying this, seven of the nine minions left the assembly.

"Gor'glon, I expect you to keep an eye on the southern kingdoms. Report anything of importance."

"Yes my Lord, your wish shall be done!"

"Tarlig, I want you to pick your four best warriors. The sticktles weakling is back; I can feel his presence. I want you to stop him before he obtains the four items of interference. Succeed, or do not return. The last of the items is hidden at Dev'ilot. You can find your triumph there. You must hurry; he is about to gain the third one. Do not fail me or your torment will out do any this world has ever seen."

"I will not fail, my Lord Sar'garian."

So, the hooded figure was my nemesis, Sar'garian. I must have given my position away by just thinking his name. He looked straight at me; it was the same skeletal face I had seen in the first dream I had after finding the ring. He snarled and waved his hand. I was instantly blinded; it felt like someone had stuck two searing red-hot pokers into my eyes. I screamed from the intolerable pain.

"What's wrong?"

Glum's voice penetrated my mind. "My eyes, the pain, I can't see!" I now had a pounding migraine. The pain was so consuming I feared I might faint. Then I heard Glum chanting. Suddenly my sight returned, but I was still in agony. "My head is killing me, is there anything you can do for me, my friend?"

"The pain will pass, be patient Tom Brown."

"Who is King Nayr Derf?" My head pounded so bad even my own voice seemed like someone yelling in my face. Glum whispered that he was the king of the largest kingdom in the western provinces.

"He is about to be attacked by the evil armies. And what is a sticktle?" When Glum described what would be equivalent to a maggot, I told him about my dream. The whole time he listened intently until I mentioned Dev'ilot, then his look of concentration turned to horror. "What's wrong?"

"Dev'ilot is the most feared place on Surrea. Only arch evil is at home there. It holds the entrance to the Abyss."

The pain finally subsided and the Tre'ton made it

apparent we had to leave.

"We must hurry, time is withering away," the Tre'ton said.

We left the Tre'ton's abode and marched back into the woods. The trees and brush in front of the Tre'ton magically moved out of his way and left a clear path for us to follow. We marched for three days, only taking time out to eat and sleep. From the day we entered Tar'loon, the forest never changed, it always looked the same. Three days after we left the Tre'ton's home, we came out of the forest to a great meadow.

In the distance I saw the tops of more of Tar'loon's great trees. The meadow was completely encircled by them, and in the middle of this huge pasture was a lake. A small lone island stood in the center of this lake with only one tree that seemed to be in the exact middle of it.

"That is The Tree of Many Names." The Tre'ton motioned towards the lonely tree. "It marks the very center of Tar'loon."

We crossed the span between the edge of the trees and the beach of the small lake. After a slight detour around a couple of creatures that looked like rabbits with two-inch fangs protruding from their mouths. Glum told me they were very fast and ferocious. He called them kilbits. The lake was so calm and clear it was eerie, at least until The Tre'ton stepped into the water, laid down and made a perfect raft.

"Climb on noble warriors."

We all climbed aboard and it took no time at all to reach the island's shore. We dismounted our living raft and waited for the Tre'ton to join us.

"Only the *One* may approach The Tree of Many Names. The rest of us must wait here."

Glum patted me on the back. "That is you Tom Brown. Go and retrieve the third item of Omens."

I left my companions standing there, knowing the future of Surrea rested in my hands. I wondered why I was doing this since it was not my world. Why did I care if this *Sar* guy was defeated or not? Even though I wished I was back at home, deep inside I felt I belonged here doing what I was doing. That something in my gut said it was my destiny, whether I liked it or not.

As I approached The Tree of Many Names. I had no idea what would happen, or what to expect. The tree was magnificent, perfect in every aspect, and brightly colored with every possible hue. A golden shine surrounded it and I stood in awe, as if I were in the presence of a God. I was about ten feet from it when it lit up like the Las Vegas strip and spoke to me.

Are you ready for the challenge, wearer of the one ring?

My knees wobbled like jello and I was not sure I could even answer. "Yes." My response sounded pathetic even to me. Now I know how Dorothy felt when she stood before the Wizard of Oz.

To pass the challenge, you must tell me my one true name. If you are the true bearer of the one ring, it will flawlessly guide you. Only one of the fruits I bear is the correct one. Pick it and eat all of it. Pick the wrong one and eternal suffering will be your prize.

The tree budded, then flowered and when the flowers withered away, fruits of all sizes and descriptions grew and ripened. All this happened in a matter of seconds. I stretched out my violently shaking hand. When I reached for a fruit I thought was the one, the ring took over and I ended up grabbing the sickest looking fruit on the awe-inspiring tree. I took a bite of it; the taste was astoundingly delicious. After quickly devouring it, my confidence grew. I felt like a superhero that could conquer any obstacle. My head started to spin and I felt giddy. Then everything went dark.

My eyes were closed, so I opened them only to find myself floating high above The Tree of Many Names. Looking down I saw myself lying in front of it with a smile across my lips. I saw Doc, Glum, Glam and the Tre'ton standing motionless by the bank. It was as if they were frozen in time.

Glum, Glam and Stum, I thought amusingly. *I wonder when Stam is going to appear?* I laughed uncontrollably.

After I regained my sanity, I realized why I was here. I had to discover the tree's true name. How I would accomplish this, I had no idea. At first, I slowly floated away from the small island. The farther I went, the faster I moved. Tar'loon's vast expanse flew by and countryside after countryside moved under my feet. I was moving so fast now, that I circled Surrea every couple of seconds, then suddenly I shot out into the darkness of space.

Planets flew by one after another, then solar systems. My speed increased with every passing second until I passed complete galaxies as if they were a tiny speck of dust. Particles of light stood still while I passed them. My head reeled from the magnitude of this astounding journey. I was so bewildered I could no longer think. The only way I can describe what happened next is by saying my mass became infinite. I found myself more or less spanning the universe. Suddenly, I felt like I was standing before several galaxies.

Why do you come before us mortal?

One of the galaxies asked me with a voice that demanded respect. "I am searching." I no longer resented nor fought the ring from taking over my being.

What makes you so insolent as to come to us for your ignorant quest? asked another.

"I am searching for the side of all that is good against that which is supreme evil."

Your quest is noble enough to consider. But, you still have not given reason enough to keep us from scattering your atoms throughout the infinite universes.

"I beg forgiveness for approaching the Gods of Space and Time, but I had no other choice. You are my only hope to stop the powers of absolute evil. They are once again making their move to gain total control over all of creation. I am The Chosen One, the redeemer. I am the only one that can stop the evil from destroying all that is good. Is this not a valid reason for approaching the true Gods with my question?"

If what you say is true, it is a valid reason. Ask your question, said the first galaxy.

"What is the true name of The Tree of Many

Names?"

In order to know your allies, you must first understand your enemies. Only then will you know the true name you seek, said the second galaxy.

Look into your own soul for the answer to your question. Go now, even our existence relies on you, said the third.

There was a blinding flash and I found myself once again in my enemy's encampment. The *one that cannot be named* was still giving orders to his Generals. I watched and listened for hours while he made battle plan after battle plan with his minions. I began to understand how crafty and deceiving my archenemy was. He never left anything to chance and always covered every angle. His strategic mind astounded me and I knew how he conquered his foes so easily. But I saw his one flaw. It shone like a large neon sign. He bullied his troops to the point of pure fear, threatening extreme suffering for the slightest mistake. Under this mask of absolute confidence, was a creature full of insecurities. I now knew my enemy like no other. He was terrified of losing.

The scene below me disappeared, replaced by a void that stretched to infinity in all directions. I felt totally and completely alone. I remembered what the God of Space and Time said; look deep into your own soul to find the answer to the question. I fought the loneliness that tried to erase my being. Then I knew I was inside my soul. It was infinitely lonely. I was my own being, my own God. I had color within my soul. I realized the answer to the question. I was ready to face all others and myself.

The answer was simple; I should have seen it long ago.

Everything spun in circles, time no longer existed. I once again felt my feet on solid ground and I opened my eyes. It was no surprise that I once again stood before the lone tree.

Are you ready to answer the challenge?

"Yes. You are The Tree of Many Names, the tree of every name. You contain the color of every creature that is or has ever been. Your true name is The Tree of Souls," I said with confidence and without the ring's help.

Only the true defender of righteousness and good would have discovered my true name. You are the rightful bearer of the one ring. You have earned the right to bear the Shield of Omens.

Upon saying this, the ground in front of me opened up. There were dirt steps leading down into the darkness under The Tree of Souls.

Before you can claim your legitimate trophy, you must give your word to never reveal my true name to anyone or anything.

"I give my word to never reveal your true name."

Do not break this promise to me, or your suffering will be absolute. Now go, take your prize and hurry to your destiny. Time grows short.

I descended into the depths under The Tree of Souls. The darkness was replaced by colors emitted from the tree's roots. There were countless wisps of colored smoke floating from one root to another, and I heard the screams of thousands of faint voices. Every once in a while, I saw a face within the confines of those transparent wisps of smoke. These must be the souls of those who have been, I decided. I walked down a long windy path and at the very end my prize glistened brightly in front of me.

A magnificent shield hung on the dirt wall. It appeared extremely heavy and made out of gold. I walked up to the lion emblem on the front and touched it with my fingers before I removed the shield from the wall. It was incredibly light, and when I wrapped my hand around the grip inside it came alive with brilliance. I also felt different inside, like I was changing into something I was not. It was hard to describe my emotions. I had never been so confused in my life. It was like an unseen force was trying to take over my very soul.

I ignored the battle that waged inside me. This was not the time to seek answers to the questions racing through my mind. Not when there was an enemy so close to its final goal. That reality was difficult to swallow. I quickly left the sanctuary of The Tree of Soul's underground tomb and bid it goodbye. I reassured the tree I knew what to do and would follow its instructions. Since time was running out, I quickly returned to my friends. This was one experience I would never forget.

Glum smiled. "That was quick."

"What do you mean?"

"You were gone only a few seconds." He looked at me inquisitively. "What happened?"

"The Tree of Many Names gave me the Shield of Omens. That's about it." It was best I kept my experiences to myself. The more I talked the easier it would be to slip and reveal the tree's true name. I could not even think it, because then Doc would know. I made a crucial promise I had to keep. I held the shield up for Glum to inspect and he smiled from ear to ear. "Glad to make you so happy."

"It is not my happiness that matters." Glum pointed to the shield. "Countless lives depend on that."

"If we are to save them, we must hurry."

The Tre'ton made it possible for us to travel back across the lake. I gave my other shield to Glam, who gladly took it and tossed his other one into the water. For some reason I sensed Sword was the only weapon I needed, so I gave the spear to Glum to store for future use. I knew Glam would rather use his sword.

I drew Sword and felt a new respect for it like I held an old friend in the palm of my hand, a friend I had used my entire life. The shield also felt at home on my arm, but I felt I was missing something, as if I was incomplete.

The Tre'ton led the way back into the forest where we traveled the rest of the day without seeing another living thing. The going seemed easier with the Tre'ton as our guide. Even the forest appeared to be at his beck and call.

When darkness fell we once again made camp. Glum conjured up another one of his excellent meals. After we ate, we sat in the dark and talked. The conversation started with old battles and went to current events while I listened intently. Then Glum asked the Tre'ton to tell me the history of Dev'ilot.

CHAPTER SEVEN

These Boots Were Not Made for Walking

"The story of Dev'ilot began at the beginning of time. The Gods were bored of being alone, so they created the universe. They populated it as they saw fit. First, they created the Tre'tons, then the humanoids and on down the line to the most insignificant entities. The humanoids began to worship the Gods and at first they liked and appreciated it, but then they had fits of jealousy over one another's worshippers. Finally, greed and corruption were born."

"The father of the Gods, Kalena, who was the first and most powerful of them, being the one who created the others, watched his children argue and fight over their mortal creations. He finally decided to construct immortals instead of destroying his children's creations. As a result, he created elves in hopes of counteracting the mortal mind with a longer living race that could learn from their mistakes. Then he brought his favorite child, Kaleno before him. He gave Kaleno as much power and wisdom as he himself possessed and told Kaleno to go and stop the bickering among his children."

"Kaleno did his father's bidding at first, but then Evil crept into him. Because of Kaleno's new wisdom and power he became tired of being a slave to his father, so he used his powers to gain the most worshippers and become the Supreme God over all. Somewhere in the process, he lost his sense of good and instead became the absolute Evil and tricked his followers into becoming the same. With each follower he gained more power until he felt strong enough to challenge his father. Then he committed the most heinous crime a God could. He killed his own brother to gain his brother's followers. This angered Kalena greatly who appeared to punish Kaleno for his crime."

"Kalena did not realize how much power Kaleno had gained and was caught by surprise. Kaleno trapped his father by putting him into a star crystal and sent him into oblivion. Kalena chastised himself for underestimating Kaleno's new powers, but even imprisoned as he was, he still had untold powers, some of which could escape the ultimate enclosure."

"From his confinement he created the nine hundred and ninety-nine levels of the Abyss and added the nine levels of Hell at the bottom. Then he used what power he had left to banish Kaleno and his followers to the ninth plane of Hell and created Dev'ilot as a one-way door into the Abyss. It was a force that attracted evil souls and pulled them into Hell.

"Over the centuries, Kaleno has succeeded in traversing the nine hundred and ninety-nine levels of the Abyss. He has worked away at the door of Dev'ilot. Even though he cannot leave the Abyss, he has broken down the door enough to allow evil to escape from it. In this way, he has once again gained an influence in the ways of the laws of the universe. This is where the *one that cannot be named* comes from. He is Kaleno's servant, and if he succeeds with his conquest, he will be able to destroy Dev'ilot, thus releasing Kaleno and all that is evil. If this happens the time of Tu'nurk will come, the end of all that exists. This includes your world as well, bearer of the one ring, so everything you hold dear is also at stake. Fail us and you fail yourself."

Glum nodded. "The time has come for rest. We leave at sunrise."

I did not have the energy to argue, so I found a patch of grass and drifted off to sleep.

I stood in the middle of a field while war waged all around me. I saw one of the beasts that was at the table with the *one that cannot be named*. He held a crowned head high above him in victory, blood dripping everywhere. I could tell the evil forces were destroying the last of their foes.

"We have succeeded and Lord Sar'garian will be pleased. Stay here Turnbol. Make sure no living creature survives. I will return to Lord Sar'garian with King Derf's head and tell him of our victory!"

The beast and his words made me sick. Once again, I floated above the evil ones' camp. The beast walked up to the evil one and bowed down on his knees. When he handed the Great Evil his war trophy the evil one laughed so loud it shook everything on the table in front of him.

"You have done well. Your efforts will not go un-rewarded. The one true God will see to that. Go now and get the armies ready for the last Great War. If we can destroy the Southern Kingdoms before the sticktles weakling can interfere, then we will be able to finally release the true God of Chaos!" Sar'garian shouted loud enough that any creature within a mile could hear.

I felt my body shake out of disgust. How could any creature be this evil? A better question was how was I supposed to stop him and his army? The job looked impossible. It was a scene from a fairytale, but where was the good fairy when you needed her to sprinkle fairy dust and make everything better?

"Ev'ekin, I want you to take three good warriors, find the weakling with the ring of interference and kill him if you can. If nothing else, slow the Tutlin up. He must not make it to Dev'ilot in time."

The creature that stood by his side appeared pleased to receive that request and he bowed to his master. The feeling of evil here was so overwhelming that it clung to me and tried to infuse itself into my body.

"Yes, my Lord Sar'garian. I will not fail you."

Glum and Glam had the last of our camp packed and was storing it away when I woke. Doc stood guard and the Tre'ton was nowhere in sight. I got up and helped them finish, then I told Glum about my dream just as the Tre'ton returned.

"The Western Kingdoms have fallen, only the great Southern Kingdoms stand between Tu'nurk and your success, warrior. Time is wilting rapidly, we must hurry. The Great Southern Kingdoms will not stand for long. The Great Evil has grown in power since the last Great War between Good and Evil."

We began our trek, traveling farther and faster in a day than we ever had before. Tension rose among us, everyone felt the new urgency to reach our goal quickly. I wondered why Glum had been so worried about entering Tar'loon. Other than the Tre'ton, the kilbits and a couple of noises, we had not seen a sign of life. I decided to inquire carefully to spare Glum's feelings. He told me the Tre'ton's were the lords of the forest.

"If it weren't for his company, we probably would have had several encounters by now. The Tre'ton can talk with all of the creatures of the woodlands and can control most of them. He has spies everywhere that tell him when danger is near and he has been leading us safely around the dangers. This is why we have not had any encounters since we met him."

Six days after my encounter with the Tree of Many Names, we arrived at the edge of Tar'loon. The Tre'ton bid us good-bye. He said he was needed in the Great Southern Kingdoms to help fight the evil horde. He was a powerful ally I hated to lose. I wished he could stay with us on our journey to Dev'ilot.

"You do not need me noble warrior. You have a strength you do not even realize you possess. Trust in yourself. You can triumph if you tap into the great power locked deep inside your soul."

I wondered if the Tre'ton had read my thoughts. "I will miss your guidance."

"You never know what the fates have in store for us. Have faith in yourself and you will be victorious."

With that last farewell we left Tar'loon and the protection of our friend and headed southeast toward Dev'ilot. The landscape was just as magnificent as any I had seen since my first look at Surrea. We traveled over flat grasslands decorated with plants of all colors and description. A large herd of the bison-like creatures moved lazily along in front of us. Glum referred to them as qualt. He explained they were very common and used for food and pelts, I guess much like earth's cows and buffalo.

In the far distance loomed a large mountain range that stretched from one horizon to the other. Somewhere high up in The Great Hor'kuth Mountains was Dev'ilot, and Glum said it would be a long and arduous journey. We traveled the rest of that day in silence. I think everyone was sullen over the loss of the Tre'ton's companionship. It was getting dark when we decided to set up camp. The Hor'kuth Mountains did not look any closer than they had when I first laid my eyes on them that afternoon.

We set up camp and went to sleep without our

normal nightly conversation. I hoped tomorrow everybody's spirits would rise.

After breakfast and breaking camp, we continued on our mission. Everyone's spirits were raised a bit, at least we were all talking and laughing again. We had marched for four hours and we were all getting tired. Then Doc stopped in his tracks and growled.

There's something amiss.

"What?" Glum asked.

I don't know. I have that uneasy feeling. The one that comes before something bad happens.

There is a trap ahead. An illusion created by our enemies.

It was the first time Sword had talked to me since we left Horzule's Keep. I had almost forgotten his ability to communicate with me. I told the others what Sword said. Suddenly the *illusion* changed from grasslands to show we were actually ten feet from the edge of a cliff, with at least a one-hundred-foot drop straight down. I sensed I was the only one in our party that saw the deadly trap. I looked at Glum. "We're headed straight for a cliff with a very long drop."

"I don't see it, but that does not surprise me."

Before I could warn Glam of the danger, we were attacked from all directions simultaneously. There was one behind us, one on both sides and a forth that was floating in the air above the illusion hiding the cliff. The creature that floated in the air resembled an orc, but taller and uglier, if that was possible. He wore black clothes similar to Asmond's and carried a staff pointed straight at me. He was floating at the same height as the ground we were all standing on. So, it looked like he was just standing there to my friends and tried to goad us to run after him since he was actually floating over the gorge.

They appeared out of thin air and took us completely by surprise. What looked like a small bolt of lightning shot out of the staff the one in the air was holding, and I instinctively ducked behind my shield. The bolt hit it and rebounded directly back to its origin. The creature's staff exploded into an enormous fireball. He was knocked backward and plummeted like a rock into the ravine. "One down. Hopefully the others would be as easy."

Glam was on my right, so I turned to face the one on the left and that is when I noticed the one approaching from behind. The three that were left all wore black plate mail, similar to knights of the thirteenth century. It was impossible to tell what they looked like, since they wore full-face helmets. Each had a different shield and helmet with a different weapon in their hand. They all rode huge horses, even bigger than Clydesdales. This was the first time I had seen a horse since I arrived in Surrea, except in my dreams.

The warrior I now faced had a brass snake coiled around his helmet with the same emblem on his large round shield. He held an immense broad sword in his massive hand. "Stand behind me Glum, Doc!" I braced myself for the onslaught. The warrior spurred his mount into action.

The beast reared up, kicked his feet around in the air, then charged. I stood my ground, kept my eye on his sword and tried to gauge where he was going to aim his stroke. He swung his shiny long weapon in an arc. I brought Sword up to meet his blow. When the two swords clashed sparks flew and Sword sheared through his like it was slicing butter. Out the corner of my eye I saw Glam fighting a warrior who had dismounted. The enemy had forced Glam toward the cliff and apparently the battle had turned against him.

The warrior I battled tossed aside his useless weapon and took off on his horse. While I watched him leave, a third fighter charged me. He was smaller than the other two and resembled Glum but was far stouter. There was an emblem of a dragon on his shield, and he wore a helmet with five tall spikes sticking out the top. He swung a large axe over his head while he charged at me.

"Glum! Go help Glam!" I prepared for the next encounter. The axe was aimed at my head, but I waited until the last second to step aside. The axe cut through the air and he thankfully missed his mark. When he passed I poked his mount in the hindquarters. The animal went crazy and threw its rider into the air. I wanted to take him out before he could recover, but I paused when Doc barked at me.

The first rider is coming back at you now!

Thanks Doc! I turned just in time to see him whip his flail while he rushed me. I did not have time to bring my shield up so I went to the ground and rolled away from his steed's hooves. I miscalculated and one of the steel tips of his weapon cut a gash in my forehead.

I jumped to my feet and wiped the blood out of my eyes with my sleeve. The one on the ground ran toward me with his axe high above his head. The other one passed him and attacked once again with his flail. I brought my shield up and when his flail struck my shield it rebounded against him with more force than his original blow. The razor-sharp spikes did nothing to his armor, but one found its way into the eye-slit in his helmet and he screamed in agony. He dropped the handle of the flail and grabbed the source of his pain.

I heard a war cry and turned to find the smaller one rushing at me, axe in hand. I blocked his strike with my shield which threw him backwards violently. I realized my shield had the property to cause a force striking it to rebound in the opposite direction with a far greater force than originally propelled it in the first place. I took advantage of the situation and jumped forward to deliver a blow to the head of my unbalanced foe.

My blow landed squarely against his helmet and it flew off into the air. He was dazed but managed to regain enough composure to block my next blow. He counter attacked again, but when his axe hit my shield it flew out of his hand. The dwarf had great fear in his ancient eyes and was now weaponless. He ran off and I let him go.

I turned to see Doc and Glum doing their best to keep the last warrior at bay. Glam and the fighter with the flail were nowhere to be seen. When the last warrior saw me rush to their aid he quickly fled.

"After him!" Glum yelled.

"Let him go, he can no longer bother us." I put my hand on Glum's shoulder to calm him down. He turned toward me with anger in his eyes.

"He'll be back. You can count on that."

"Where's Glam?"

"He was forced over the cliff by the dirt bat that just ran with his wings folded behind him."

His answer was filled with sarcasm and I could not blame him a bit. "Let's go get him. Got a rope in that bag?" Glum pulled out a long rope and we secured it around Doc and carefully lowered him down to the bottom. Then Glum and I navigated the steep rock cliff down into the ravine. There we found the charred remains of a creature Glum referred to as an *Ogre magician*, who lay bundled up next to our companion. Glam was unconscious, but still breathing. His leg had a compound fracture and blood oozed from his nose and mouth. Glum went over to him and pulled out his book. He told me it would take longer than usual because of Glam's wounds.

Doc stood watch and I looked over the charred corpse. Everything on the body was burnt to a crisp, except for a dagger and his leather boots. Out of curiosity, I took off the boots and noticed his feet were also burnt.

"How did his feet burn when his boots aren't even singed?"

"Because they are elven."

I turned toward the familiar voice behind me. Asmond was floating six feet in the air with his legs crossed in a sitting position, not more than seven feet from where I stood. I felt my anger grow. "You! If it weren't for you I would not be here!"

"If it was not for the ring."

"Thanks for correcting me. I wish I had never

found the accursed thing!"

"You didn't find it, the ring found you. You are the descendant of Sterling the Great. You are the Savior."

"I don't want to be!" My anger grew to new heights and I wanted to punch him.

"You have no choice. You are the bearer of the one ring. If you fail this world, you fail all worlds. Until you successfully complete the quest that has befallen you, the ring will not come off. Even if it did, you would not have a world to return to if *the one that cannot be named* triumphs."

"Until the ring leaves your possession of its own free will, no power in the universe can return you to your earth. You must accept your destiny."

"I won't…." Asmond disappeared into thin air before I could finish my sentence. Once again, the battle raged inside me. I did not want to accept the so-called heritage that had been thrown at me. I did not ask for this, so why was I here? Why did their war become my war?

I sat down and decided I was not going to go on, yet something deep inside told me I was born for this war. It was my destiny to stop the great evil. Somehow, I knew I was the only one that could fix this problem, regardless of how I felt. The question was, "Did I care?" Just then Doc spoke.

If what Asmond says is true, you have no choice, Tom. You have to beat the evil or everything you hold dear will be lost and we will never see our home again.

But what if I can't? What if I lose to the bum? I may not be good enough to beat him. I not only doubted my abilities right now, but I also doubted my sanity. Then Doc's voice jumped in again.

According to everything we have been told, the ring knows you can. It picked you to succeed where no other could. Besides, I believe you can. I hope what I think matters to you.

A new confidence surged inside me and I wanted to succeed. I was ready to win this challenge destiny brought me. I jumped up with a new inner strength, ready to continue the quest. "Are you guys ready to go?"

Glam was up now, with only a slight limp to show for his mishap. Glum looked weak and pale, but said he was ready. We carefully climbed up the other side of the ravine. I held the rope to the makeshift harness that would pull Doc up when I reached the top. Poor Doc could not hang onto the rocks like we could.

We continued our trek across the barren countryside. While we walked I mentioned the dagger and boots I commandeered from the Ogre mage. I gave Glum the dagger and he told me to put the boots on. I looked at them and realized they were too small for my foot, but Glum insisted I try anyway.

We stopped long enough for me to try and put them on and tie them securely on my feet. Just as soon as I stuck my foot into the boot, it seemed to adjust to my shoe size and was a perfect fit. They were the most comfortable shoe I had ever worn, to the point it seemed like I could walk miles and not even feel like I had gone but a few feet.

"Try jumping." Glum stated.

I jumped my normal distance a few times.

"Try running."

I ran at full speed, to my surprise I covered four times the distance I would in the same amount of time. I now moved at the speed of a racehorse. I tried to stop and fell flat on my face. The force I hit the ground with knocked me silly and nearly unconscious.

After I stood, all I could do was stare at the wondrous boots in amazement like a child with a new toy. I committed myself to master the things with a conviction. Every once in a while, I would land on my face. By the end of the day I had gotten pretty good. After a couple of days, I could run sideways, backwards, and finally I was able to do a somersault at full speed.

We covered a lot of ground in the next four days and were grateful our last encounter was at the ravine and we had not had one since. We were marching along at a good speed, then Doc stopped abruptly.

I sense the same three minds we fought a few days ago not far in front of us.

A couple of seconds later the three warriors saw us and lined up to bar our passage. Their three horses were tethered to the stump of a long dead tree several feet behind them. The enemy stood with their weapons drawn, ready for battle. One had a bow, the other two held swords.

"Glam and I will deal with them; you two stay back and help us if we need you."

Glam and I approached the three fighters and the one in the middle stepped forward.

"Give up your quest or die!"

"I think you are the ones who should give up." These guys were good at hiding their emotions because I saw no change in their expressions. Glam stood beside me so I leaned toward him. "Stay behind me until I tell you to attack." He moved behind me.

"There are only three of you this time and no illusions to hide behind. I will give you one more chance to withdraw or suffer the wrath of Sterling the Great!" I could not believe I said the last part, but it did shake them up a little.

The man with the longbow tapped it on the ground. "The only one that will suffer is you!"

Two arrows flew at me, which was why I told Glam to get behind me. My Shield was ready to block the oncoming projectiles. The first one flew straight and true, but I had to raise my shield slightly above my head to catch the second one. Just as expected, the arrows returned to their origin. The first one caught him in his helmet and knocked him slightly backwards. The arrows couldn't penetrate his thick body metal. The second struck perfectly between his helmet and armor, piercing the thin chain mail protecting his neck and buried itself deep in his throat. He slumped to the ground and clutched the shaft that protruded from his fatal wound. The other two circled around to attack our flanks.

"Glam, take the one on the right!" I moved to intercept the one coming from the left. I really wanted him since he was the one who forced Glam over the edge of the cliff. He had the emblem of a skeleton on his rectangular shield. There was a dragon curled around his helmet, with the head resting on top and the wings sticking out the right side of the helmet, protecting an ear.

I ran at normal speed, but when I was within twenty feet of him I switched to the boots full potential. Since he had readied himself for my assault, I jumped into a somersault over his head and caught him by surprise. When I was directly over him, I swung down with Sword and sliced into his shoulder. After I landed behind him I jumped to my feet and turned to face my opponent. The blow I dealt him did not faze him a bit, even though his armor had a deep gash and blood flowed freely from it. "Yield or die!"

"I will never yield to a sticktle!"

He charged and I stood ready. He swung his sword and used his shield like a battering ram. Luckily, I had seen this move before, or it would have caught me by surprise. His sword rebounded off my shield which threw him off balance, and he stumbled by me then fell. With no time to waste I buried Sword into his back as he was trying to get up and the tip of Sword emerged out the front plate of his armor. He fell back to the ground and twitched with the spasms of death. I started to pull Sword out of the body when I heard a battle cry behind me. At the same time, I heard Doc yelling at me.

Watch out behind you, Tom!

I turned just in time to see a sword coming straight at my neck. Luckily, I had the shield in place since I was weaponless. His sword hit my shield and nearly knocked me over. To my dismay, it did not rebound against him. I braced myself for the return swing. It nearly pulled the shield from my grasp. I decided to experiment, evidently there was a reason I felt the blows against my shield. Since I had received the shield from The Tree of Many Names this was the first blow I had felt.

I grabbed Sword's hilt with my right hand while I waited for the third blow that sped toward me. This time it hit and I did not feel the blow. My opponent was caught off-guard, unprepared for the recoil. He found himself on the ground and weaponless as I watched his sword fly out of his hand and through the air. Out of desperation he jumped to his feet and charged me with his shield. Without letting go of Sword, I leveled my shield and braced myself for the living battering ram. I did not feel a thing when his shield struck mine. He flew backwards through the air just like Glam had when the giant hit him with its club.

He hit the ground hard and rolled. He lost his wind and had great difficulty getting up. This gave me time to free Sword from the corpse. It took all my strength to retrieve my weapon. With one final tug I victoriously held Sword in my hand where it belonged.

The warrior was on his feet again and I moved within striking distance. He was now completely defenseless since his sword and shield were both more than ten feet from his grasp. He went down on his knees and pathetically begged for mercy.

Glum, Glam and Doc ran to my side. Doc and I wanted to let him go, if he swore to renounce his allegiance to the evil one. Glam would not hear of it since it was the second time this bunch had severely harmed him. Glum also did not believe he would follow such an oath. In the end, I gave into Glum's greater wisdom, since he had been right about everything so far.

Reluctantly I turned to walk away. With my back to the nervous warrior, I heard Glam's sword whistle through the air then strike the fighter, I winced when the warrior let out a final death scream. It was the first-time death had bothered me since I set foot on Surrea and for a couple of weeks after I had a hard time sleeping. I could not stop dreaming about that horrible scream.

After checking the bodies for anything of worth, the only thing we kept was a bow and a few arrows which Glum put in his bag. Glam did take a fancy to the winged dragon helmet of the last fighter, tossing his aside he adorned his newest prize. The horses were a welcome sight to our weary feet and made traveling much easier as we continued on our journey.

CHAPTER EIGHT

The Challenge of the Elements

We traveled for eight days without an encounter and finally arrived at the first foothills of The Great Hor'kuth Mountains. At first the going was easy, but then we arrived at the steeper hills that had deep gorges and rocky cliffs which we maneuvered around. Then we stopped at the edge of a deep, long, and wide ravine which made the Grand Canyon look like a minor crack in the ground.

The gigantic canyon appeared to go on forever in both directions. We decided it would take longer to go around it than cross it. With great sadness we freed the horses. Glum grabbed his bag and pulled out what he called mountain climbing gear. Luckily, I had done some climbing before I became a fitness instructor. My karate sensei told me it was a good way to learn balance and gain control within, but I never used equipment this primitive before. This would be a challenge.

First, we lowered Glam down to a ledge roughly two hundred feet below. Then we wrapped Doc in pelts to protect him from the ragged cliff side. Glam untied Doc and I pulled the rope back so I could lower Glum. Once Glum was safe I began my descent down the ragged cliff. It took all the experience of my past climbs to maneuver down to my companions. Crude or not, I had little choice if we were to succeed in our quest, besides it took no time at all to master such barbaric equipment. We repeated this procedure forty-nine times before we reached a slope at the bottom that was level enough to traverse without ropes.

The ravine's bottom was so wide and rugged, it took five days to cross before we arrived at our next climbing challenge. The incredibly tall, insurmountably looking cliff face convinced us to make camp and wait until morning to tackle the task that was before us. We each thanked our own Gods for allowing us to make it this far and prayed we would make it the rest of the way. We ate then bedded down, each of us fighting the depression of the drudgery before us in our own way.

Once again, I found myself above my enemies' encampment, only this time instead of a war council, I watched some kind of ceremony. There was a guy jumping around a large fire that looked like the witch doctor in my first dream of Surrea. *The one that cannot be named* stood in the middle of the fire with his hands raised to the sky chanting. He was completely engulfed in the flames. The fire danced around his body, yet caused no apparent damage.

He had complete control of the fire as flames jumped from his fingertips into the night sky. There were at least fifty hooded figures sitting in a wide circle around the bonfire chanting in unison with the evil one. Every once in a while, a face made out of flames could be seen within the fire. All at once the chanting stopped and the fire disappeared.

"The sticktles weakling will have his hands full with the elementals! Tomorrow we start the final assault against the last obstacle in the way of our total victory. This time our master shall not be denied his rightful supreme control of all of existence. We will regain his kingdom, or our suffering will know no equal. We cannot, we must not fail him. Go now and rest. We march at the first light!"

I woke to see my friends sleeping, but the evil one's voice was still in my head. Doc stood guard next to the small dying fire in the center of our camp. I was beginning to understand my dreams, I realized this one was a warning of what was about to happen.

What's wrong Tom?

Wake up Glum and Glam quick, were about to be attacked!

I now understood the warning in my dream. Doc woke both of them up and I asked Glum what an elemental was. I stood and readied myself for battle as both of them rose from a dead sleep. Before Glum could answer, the fire behind me flared up and made sounds like a flame thrower. When I turned I came face to face with a creature made of transparent flames. He had the shape of a humanoid. but his eyes and mouth were the only parts of the huge body I could not see through. It was the first time since I arrived on this phenomenal planet that I had known absolute fear. I felt like running and nearly dropped Sword when I stumbled backwards from the terrifying sight.

Then the ground shook. I heard a rumble off to my right, like the sound several boulders made when they tumbled down a hillside. A quick glance showed nothing.

Glum pointed at the fire being. "That is a fire elemental." Then he pointed toward the hill. "And that is an earth elemental."

Not wanting to take my eyes off the fire creature standing in front of me, I did not look to see the other one.

"I am Sg'ninnej Yaj, ruler of the Golden Fire Pool. I have been sent, along with my elemental brother by Sar'garian to challenge the one warrior fighting for the side of all that is good against the side of all that is evil. Which of you is the one true champion?"

The fire monster had a magical voice which made me hesitate as total fear set in. I tried to muster what little confidence I could and hoarsely answered the creature. "I... am the one." I fought just to get those words to leave my lips.

"Noble warrior of the one ring, are you ready to accept the challenge of the elements?"

"Glum, what is he talking about?"

"I don't know Tom Brown. I have never actually

seen any of the elementals before. I have only heard of them, and very little at that. However, I do know it can be killed."

"I am waiting warrior. Do you accept?"

Glam started to advance on the creature. "We kill! No need challenge."

"Stop Glam. This is my fight." Glam reluctantly stepped back.

"Explain the challenge of the elements." I demanded as I started to regain my composure.

"If you accept, you will fight four champion elementals, one from each of the four elemental pools, one at a time, one on one. If something tries to interfere during the challenge, or you do not accept the challenge, then all the elementals from all the pools will come and fight. We are a noble race and it is against our laws to break the challenge once it has been accepted by either side."

"I have no choice then, I must accept your challenge!" I braced myself for the inevitable battle.

"The challenge has been accepted. Prepare to die, warrior! Fire was the first of the elements to exist and the first to fight."

The fire being advanced on me and I had no idea how to fight it, or what would kill it. I relied on my shield and sword. I decided to charge and attack first, before it had a chance to attack me. I swung, but the thing moved surprisingly fast and dodged my attack. It took a swipe with his fist, but I blocked it with my shield. I was elated when the shield had the same effect on the fire elemental that it had on everything else. The elemental's fist struck my shield and rebounded hard, throwing the thing off balance. I took the initiative and brought Sword down.

The elemental howled in pain and swiped at me with his other hand. The blow caught me in the shoulder, burning into my skin and bowling me over. He came at me, lifted his foot to stomp on my head while I was down. I brought my shield up in time to stop his fiery foot from hitting my face. It bounced off the shield and practically lifted the elemental off the ground. I managed to jump up just when the creature went down.

The tables had turned and I wasted no time. I brought Sword down on its fiery leg and severed it from the beastly thing. The elemental sat up and took a swipe at me while it screamed in pain. I brought Sword up to block his swing and severed his hand at the wrist. The elemental withered in extreme agony on the ground. Then I brought Sword down for the final blow across his chest and cut the thing in half. He dissipated into thin air. Then a deep voice resounded behind me.

"Fire was first, then came earth. I am Dirtclod, ruler of the Magma Pool, being the second of the four elements. I am your next challenge. Prepare to die, human!"

I now faced an elemental made of dirt and rock, and like the first, it also had the shape of a humanoid. This one was very solid, but blended into the rocky hillside so well, it was hard to find when it was not moving.

Once again, I took the initiative and rushed the being. Before I could reach him, even with the aid of the magic boots, he bent over and dug his massive hands into the ground. He pulled the ground up just before I was within striking distance. It was like he literally pulled a rug out from underneath me.

I flipped into the air and fell flat on my back. I started to get up, but he hit me in the chest. I flew through the air and landed on my back again. I felt like someone just clobbered me with a large baseball bat. I had trouble breathing and worked to catch my breath. Without a doubt I had a broken rib or two. I heard the elemental's heavy footsteps approaching and waited for him to strike.

He lifted his huge foot above my head. Once he committed himself to the attack and began to bring his foot down, I shoved the shield between him and my head. His foot hit and bounced off my shield. That gave me the opportunity to take a swipe at his other leg with Sword. To my surprise, I swung at him with a mace. I know I had Sword in my hand a second ago and had not let go, so how could I have this unknown weapon in my hand? The mace struck the elemental's leg. Between my blow and the rebound properties of the shield, he went down hard. I got to my feet and pain shot through my side and caused me to breathe hard. My vision blurred as I watched the elemental start to get up.

I imagine he wasn't very bright because as he rose the rock-being took his eyes off me and gave me the perfect opportunity to club him in the head. I swung with all my might, the blow caught him in the temple and I heard his neck snap. He slumped to the ground, melted into it and completely disappeared.

"Two down, who's next?" I yelled in triumph.

The wind picked up, and I heard a roar like an ocean wave crashing over reefs. Then a large wave of water with eyes and a mouth came toward me. It stopped and stared at me.

"Fire was the first, second was earth, and then came water. I am Slosh of the Tidal Wave Pool, third of the four elements; I am your next challenge. Prepare to die, human!"

I fought a being of fire and one made of rocks, but how do you fight a wave of water?

"You know Slosh, your two friends said the same thing, and now they are in elemental heaven. Are you ready to join them? When I'm done with you, your name is going to be Slush of the Itsy-Bitsy Pool."

"You dare mock a water elemental, slig! Defend yourself; I am going to squash your puny human frame."

That was all it took for the elemental to come at me. This opponent had no physical means of propulsion, no legs. He glided across the ground without leaving a trail of any kind. I braced myself and wondered how it attacked? How could I defend myself? I did not have to wait very long. While it approached, an arm of water came out of the wall that now towered over me. The arm moved fast and struck me in the chest. I flew backward head over heels and landed face down in a patch of grass.

This was starting to become a habit, and I did not like it. My sides felt like jello, and my ribs were killing me. It was all I could do to keep from passing out. Then the roar of my newest opponent said he was not done with me. There was not enough time to get up so I decided to use the tactics that had worked on my last adversary. I rolled over, brought my shield up to block the elemental's next blow.

Once again, I held sword in my other hand, and I realized it must be able to change into different weapons if needed. Later, I found out the rock elemental could only be hurt by a mace.

Use the shield to protect your upper body and head, and when it comes down on you, stick me straight up into the air to impale it. I will do the rest.

The elemental towered above me. I readied Sword and buried my head under my shield. Then my opponent made his move and crashed down with all its force. I gripped Sword tight and jabbed it straight up into the wall of water. An ear-piercing scream consumed me as water came crashing down around me. I was now lying in a puddle of water and the water creature was no longer there.

Getting up was no easy task. I grabbed my side in pain and had difficulty breathing. I was completely soaked and my head was dizzy. When I thought I could walk without passing out, I took one step, as a loud roar stopped me in my tracks. It was the sound of a tornado in the distance. The wind turned so strong it sent dust and small objects flying everywhere.

I wondered if I would survive this last challenge. My thoughts were jumbled, and my ribs hurt so bad I could no longer feel the second degree burn on my shoulder. I propped myself up with Sword to keep from being knocked over by the wind.

All you have to do is touch it with me, and I will do the rest.

Fire, rock and water, what was next, lightning? Then I saw a small funnel cloud form in front of me. It was roughly eight feet tall and about a foot wide at its base and four feet at its top. It reminded me of a dust devil in a field, except this one had eyes and a mouth.

"Fire was first, second was earth, third was water, and then came air. I am Whirl of the Storm Pool, the last of the four elements. I am your final challenge. Prepare to die, human!"

I was beginning to hate the words, *prepare to die human*. The way I felt at the moment, that statement could become reality. Sword said to just touch it with him. Sounded easy enough, but tornadoes were very unpredictable, and as I was about to find out so was this one.

It moved much quicker than the other three elementals, too fast to out-run it, even if I was fresh, going at the fastest speed my magic boots would allow. Then it came at me. I did as Sword said and shoved it straight up into thin air. The creature hopped over my head and landed behind me. Before I could turn it hit me in the back and knocked me flat on the ground. I rolled as it landed right where I had just been.

I swung again and sliced through thin air. It hopped up and came down toward my chest. I jerked the shield between the two of us. It hit the shield and bounced back up into the air. Instead of coming back down for another attack, the accursed thing hovered above me evidently waiting for me to get up. It became a waiting game I was determined to win. It hovered four feet over me while I remained with my back on the ground, shield ready and Sword in hand. It seemed like an eternity we waited for each other to move first.

"Get up and fight sticktle!" It goaded me.

"Why don't you come down and get me, you bag of hot air." I guess it didn't like being called that because the thing growled then attacked. Trying to time it perfectly, I rolled out from underneath it and held Sword out right where I judged the elemental would hit. I looked just as the surreal creature landed straight on top of Sword. Just as soon as the elemental touched Sword it looked like it was being sucked into a vacuum cleaner and thus ended my challenge. I tried to get up and as my adrenaline *rush* left me, everything went black.

It was the middle of the afternoon when I opened my eyes to bandages on my chest and pain everywhere. Sword was sheathed, lying next to me with my shield. I tried to get up and, nearly passed out. I let out a painful scream then laid back down.

"About time great warrior woke up." Glam walked to my side.

"Where's Glum?" I winced from the effort it took just to ask the question.

"Me not know. Not here when fight end."

Glam looked worried. Before I could ask him another question, Doc jumped up and licked my cheek. I petted his head. *Glad to see you too.*

Tom, something grabbed Glum during your fight. I didn't detect its presence until after it had taken him. I would have followed them, but I couldn't find a trail. I have no idea what it was, but I sensed great evil. Rest now. There is nothing we can do until you're well enough to travel. I wanted to argue, but knew it was futile, so I allowed myself to drift back off to sleep.

I was watching myself fight the water elemental and from this vantage point it gave me a new perspective on what I did wrong. On the first attack I had the wrong stance, my shield was not positioned correctly, so I was not prepared for the blow.

I tried to warn myself about the blow, but it did not reach my other self's conscious mind. The attack came and knocked me over, something above the scene caught my attention. I looked up and saw a huge bird that looked like a bald eagle, only it was as large as a 747 Jumbo Jet. It swooped down and grabbed Glum from behind with such force it knocked him unconscious. There was no way for him to tell anyone about his abduction.

When the creature rose back into the sky with Glum, his black bag fell out of his tunic, plummeted to the ground and landed in the middle of a thick bush hidden from sight. I floated behind to see where it might land. It flew only a short distance and disappeared into a cave located along the side of the ravine's cliff. I followed it into the cave to make sure Glum was okay.

The creature put Glum in a cage made of various kinds of bones. This bird creature evidently had intelligence because it used a key to lock the skeletal cage. It turned around and headed straight at me. I was defenseless. I had no weapons, no shield. I tried to move out of its way, but it ignored me as it rushed toward me. I covered my face as the creature trampled me, but there was no impending crash of its body smashing into mine. Then it simply flew out of the cave opening. There was no way it could have gotten by me without trampling me; there just was not enough room. I quit thinking about the beast and turned my thoughts back to setting Glum free.

"I am glad you're alright, I'll have you out in just a few seconds."

Either he was delirious or I was dreaming again, because he didn't seem to realize I was there, nor did he acknowledge me. I reached for the lock on the cage and my hands went right through it. This must be a dream, I decided to hurry back to my camp. Maybe my subconscious was with this dream body, and my physical body could not wake up until my dream body returned to it. I took no chances. I returned to camp and merged back with my physical body.

CHAPTER NINE

The Valley of the Damned

Waking up I yelled for Doc and Glam, they came running to me and I explained what had happened. I guided Doc to the bush where the black bag lay hidden while Glam built a stretcher to carry me on. Glam was anxious to hit the trail so we could retrieve Glum.

I bounced down the trail in the contraption Glam built. He was an exceptional wood carver, constructing this wheel barrel-type litter that he easily controlled himself, and with only an axe to work with.

It took the rest of the afternoon to travel the half mile to the cave entrance. Glam was nearly exhausted, since he had to lift Doc and me up and down a series of small cliffs we had to cross. Glam insisted on climbing the rocky cliff free hand and said he had no need for civilized equipment. Doc and I watched for the possible return of the giant eagle, while Glam scaled the cliff.

After several tries, I finally pulled the bow and arrows out of Glum's amazing black bag. It was difficult for me to move, but I ignored the pain and did what had to be done. I sheathed Sword, laid my shield across my lap, and watched the sky with the bow in hand. I glanced up the cliff, amazed at how Glam climbed like a pro, even in the waning light. After Glam disappeared into the cave's darkness, I saw the giant bird. I looked at Doc. *Can you contact Glam?*

I'm in contact with him now.

Warn him of the bird's return. I let two arrows fly, ignoring the extreme pain that shot through me for the effort. One arrow buried itself in a wing; the other flew past missing the bird completely. It was like a pin prick to the great avian, but it still drew its attention to me. The wing span of the thing had to be at least three hundred feet, each of its curved talons were the size of my arm, and the beak was large enough to easily swallow me whole.

It swooped toward us and I felt like a sitting duck. I shot three more arrows before it attacked; one hit it in the body, another hit the wing and the third missed. My arrows were less that pin pricks to the beast. All I did was anger the thing even more. I threw down the bow, drew Sword and grabbed my shield just before the gigantic claws reached for me.

I was standing now, swinging Sword back and forth while the creature hovered above me and waited for an opening. The giant bird misjudged its swoop and lost a claw for the effort. It made a deafening screech and flew away at an extraordinary speed. That's when I noticed I had been standing and fighting. I fainted from the overwhelming pain that entered my consciousness.

I had no idea how long I had been out, but when I woke, it was the middle of the night, two of Surrea's three moons shone brightly in the night sky. Doc stood guard while Glum and Glam slept.

Doc explained how Glam had climbed down to get Glum's bag and then scaled the cliff again in the dark. Using the gear, they ascended back down and made camp. Glum retired not long ago after healing my injuries.

I jumped up feeling new and refreshed with no signs of my recent wounds. Being wide awake I told Doc to get some rest, and I would stand guard. The rest of the night I reflected back on my experiences since the night I first put on the Ring of Omens.

Morning arrived and I admired another of Surrea's spectacular sunrises, each one as magnificent as the last. Since one sun followed right behind the other they produced fabulous results. I relaxed while I admired the morning's sunrise, at least until our friend the giant eagle returned. I stood and brandished Sword while the creature circled high above.

Evidently the feathered monster did not want to mess with the tiny beings far below that could deliver such a vicious bite, because it flew into its cave and disappeared into the dark depths. A few seconds later I heard a faint screech of anguish when it realized its morning meal had escaped. This was the last time I would ever see one of the huge avian monsters.

Glum conjured breakfast while I woke Glam and Doc. "Come on guys. We've lost a precious day and need to make up the time, so hustle." They hurried over to eat, then we all broke camp. Glam scaled the cliff wall once again. This time he went to the top and secured the two hundred feet of rope to a large tree that grew by the ledge. When he threw it down, the rope barely made it to the ground. I wrapped Doc in the usual way and Glam hauled him up. Glum went next and I followed.

The farther we traveled into the Hor'kuth Mountains the rougher the terrain became. I realized how the great Hor'kuth got its name. It had become necessary to make a backpack I could use to strap Doc to my back, since my canine friend could not traverse the dangerous terrain. This of course made it harder for me, and even Glam was having difficulty.

We relied on the primitive gear in order to scale the perilous cliffs. We climbed for days and it seemed we were getting nowhere fast. The only living creatures we encountered during our ascent was Surrea's equivalence to a mountain goat. The higher we climbed, the colder it became and the more pelts we had to wear to keep warm.

When we reached snow, our climb slowed to a crawl. My fingers and toes felt completely frozen, and I sensed the end of our quest was near. As cold as we all were, we could not get there soon enough. Each day it became more difficult to find a place to sleep. It got to a point where we had to huddle together just to keep from freezing to death at night. Sleep was hard to come by. Nothing went right when you were so cold you shook so bad you could not see straight. I got to the point I was fearful of losing my fingers and toes to frostbite.

I was first in line to top the ridge. and if anything waited for us I was ready. When I pulled myself up I found a very unexpected sight, there was a valley that stretched as far as I could see which looked like a gigantic bowl cut into the top of the mountain peak. The valley was rich with vibrant green vegetation and had a haze which circled the mountain top that seemed to protect it from the freezing cold. Even the snow that was currently falling did not touch the placid scene.

This wall of haze was ten feet in front of me and partially obscured my vision of the valley beyond it. I could see a solitary mountain in the center of the valley far off in the distance, standing like a lonely sentinel watching over its territory. While I looked at it I thought I saw the mountain erupt like a volcano, but I was not sure because of the haze in front of me. Just then my companions joined me.

Glum walked up and stood next to me. "That is the land of Vect, otherwise known as the Valley of the Dead or Damned. No intelligent being on the side of what is good would dare enter the haze boundary. That mountain in the center is where Dev'ilot is located. I am told, they call it Niat'nuom Live. Our quest leads there so we must enter the accursed place."

Even though we were freezing to death, no one seemed to be in a hurry to enter the Valley of the

Dammed. Since we were quickly running out of time, we reluctantly stepped into the haze, and I immediately felt like I had stepped into a time machine that threw me back to the prehistoric era. We went from extreme cold to blistering hot, and the shock to my senses practically knocked me out. I turned around to look at the wall of haze and found a rock wall instead. Out of curiosity, I reached out to touch the wall. Instead of solid rock my hand went through it and I felt frigid cold on the other side.

We quickly peeled off our winter protection, which had actually shielded us from the heat. It took some time for my body to adjust. My hands and feet came alive with pain. I let Doc out of his protective carrier, since we were once again on flat plains and he no longer needed the warmth we wrapped around him. We worked our cold stiff joints until they were as close to normal as possible. We rubbed our fingers and toes and thought about the next leg of our journey.

I viewed the unusual scene more clearly now. Like all the other landscapes I had seen on Surrea, it was alive with brilliant color. Except it looked more like a scene from a dinosaur movie. The plants were massive, larger than I guessed was normal for Surrea. Even the trees were larger than the giants in Tar'loon, plus I thought I saw what looked like a pterodactyl in the distance. I could see our goal, Dev'ilot and it had large streams of lava flowing from its top, proving it was volcanic.

From Glum and Glam's expressions I could tell they were as amazed by the scenery as I was and were reluctant to enter the unique region. However, we had come this far and I for one was not going to quit now. I sensed the armor of Omens was close, drawing me to it and felt it was urgent I find it as soon as possible.

"Let's go." I started down the gradual incline. Doc came to my side, Glum and Glam followed close behind. We marched into the valley with a marked determination to successfully complete our quest. The farther we went into the Valley of the Damned the hotter it became, and the thicker the vegetation. It started to look like the middle of the Amazon forest. We traveled for three days without an encounter. On the fourth day, we ate breakfast and broke camp in the usual manner. We were just getting ready to continue the journey when Doc, who was on guard as usual, warned of the approach of several beings.

There's something coming straight at us from up ahead. More behind, wait, we're surrounded. They're going to attack!

I started to move toward Glum who was in the middle of the small clearing of our camp and was about to yell for Doc and Glam, but before I could warn them something or someone clubbed me in the back of the head. Everything went dark.

CHAPTER TEN

Falling in Love over a Sword

My head hurt terribly, like the worst hangover I've ever had. I opened my eyes to find myself completely naked, lying on a bed of dirt, leaves, and grass. I was inside a large cage made of tree branches and twine. Glum and Glam were imprisoned with me. They were sound asleep. It was the middle of the night, and there was a bonfire in the middle of a large crude camp. Not a creature stirred anywhere. I tried to move and realized my hands and feet were securely bound.

It's about time you came to.

Doc! What happened? Where are you? I was afraid something happened to you.

I'm behind you in the brush. I've been hiding here waiting for you to recover. Glumstron doctored you up, but said that due to the nature of your injury you would probably be out for some time. As far as what happened, we were attacked by several creatures that Glum referred to as Hill Giants. They threw several small boulders in their attack and one of them hit you in the back of the head. They captured Glum and Glam. I barely escaped. I followed them and watched where they put our gear. So far, I've counted seventeen.

Seventeen! We barely survived two giants. How are we going to fight seventeen of them?

They are much smaller and weaker than the two you fought before. Glam killed three before they got him. If we can recover our gear you'll have the shield you didn't have when you fought those other two giants

Doc, you'll have to help us get out of this cage and recover our gear. Then we'll worry about the giants.

I braced myself and mustered all my strength and strained against my bonds. At first they did not budge, but then they started to stretch and finally snapped. I quickly untied my feet then scooted over to unbind Glum and Glam who opened their eyes when I touched them. I released Glum and proceeded to find a way out of our crude prison while Glum unbound Glam. I came to the conclusion that in order to get through the wood bars, I was going to have to make quite a bit of noise.

How far away is our gear, Doc?

Not very. It's in a wood hut on the other side of the fire. The hut is about the same distance from the fire as you are.

Since we were about forty feet from the fire, the hut was around eighty, too far to go without being caught if the giants were anywhere near.

Do you know how close the nearest giant is?

There's several lying just outside the fire's light.

Do you think you can get inside the shack, and get my boots and Glum's black bag?

I can try. I'll be right back.

Several tense minutes passed slower than I thought possible. Glum, Glam, and I sat helplessly waiting for Doc. Without weapons we did not stand a chance in a confrontation against the giants. Finally, Doc returned successfully brandishing the items in his mouth. I grabbed for the two items I had requested just as a giant came into the light and caught us in the act. He let out a loud cry of alarm. The time for silence was over! I tossed the bag to Glum, ripped open the cage and quickly put on the magic boots.

"Give me the spears!" I shouted at Glum as I stood up. He quickly responded and I grabbed the four spears he was holding and once again stood ready for action. Glam grabbed the bow, and had a sword lying at his feet ready if needed. Even Glum held his mace in his hand prepared to fight if necessary. I jumped through the opening I had made, and headed toward the hut that contained my clothes, Sword and my shield. A horde of nine-foot giants rushed into the firelight.

With a spear in hand, I reared back and threw it at the closest giant between me and the shack. He fell to his knees and clutched the shaft that protruded from his chest. I stopped and threw two more spears at two other giants that ran toward me side by side. One spear hit the giant's hip, and the other spear hit the second giant in the shoulder. I heard a yell behind me and turned just in time to see a crude club coming straight for my head. Not having enough time to react, all I saw was the look of anger in the giant's eyes while the club moved in slow motion toward me. An instant before the club made contact the giant stiffened, his smile disappeared and his gaze turned to despair.

The club fell to the ground along with the giant. He landed face down to show two arrows protruding from his back. I saw Glam still in the cage with a smile on his lips. I gave him a thankful nod for having my back. Now only two giants stood between me and my weaponry. With luck I could avoid them.

These giants were slow and did not seem too bright. I figured tricking them might be easy. I ran toward them at a normal speed and waited for the right moment then kicked my boots into high gear. I ran between one of them and the fire, dodging a club as I dashed by. There was now nothing between me and the shack as I quickly out distanced the two giants running after me.

I made my way to the wood hut and ran inside, quickly surveying its contents. In the far corner I spotted our gear and I headed straight for it. I picked up my shield and started tossing items aside looking for Sword. I frantically searched and was ready to rip the entire hut apart when the two giants entered. I momentarily gave up my search and grabbed Glam's sword from the floor in front of me then turned my attention to my two adversaries.

My need to find Sword was so great I rushed the giants recklessly. I chopped one's head off and buried the sword in the other one's chest before either of them could react. I quickly got dressed and then returned to the back of the hut to search for Sword. I became frantic because without Sword it seemed I was missing a part of myself.

I tore the hut apart but did not find Sword. Suddenly I sensed I dropped it when the rock hit me in the head and no one noticed, actually it was more like I knew. I stopped my search and returned to the present reality. I had left my friends to defend themselves, and my senseless search may have cost them their lives. I pulled Glam's sword from the giant's chest and raced out of the shack.

The scene before me was not good. Glum had his back to a tree and held three giants at bay. Glam fought five of the creatures and they were slowly backing him into the fire. I ran to aid Glum, striking one of Glam's assailants in the back as I passed by him. I figured Glum was less likely to survive his adversaries' attacks than Glam so I rushed to his aid. Besides, if Glam died, Glum had the ability to bring him back to life, so the choice was obvious.

I came at them from behind as quickly and quietly as possible. I used a running jump kick and slammed into the one furthest left of Glum and still managed to take a swing at the one next to it in the middle. Since I paid more attention to my kick, the sword missed its target, but my kick struck home with all the force I could muster and knocked the giant down. Since I was not used to doing Karate kicks with magic boots on, I lost my balance and landed flat on my back in front of the giant I swung the sword at. He took advantage of the opportunity and brought his wooden club down toward my chest. I reacted as fast as I could and maneuvered my shield into place. His club struck it and I felt the full force of the blow. I countered, by slicing his leg off at the knee. The giant hollered, let out a blood-curdling scream then fell face-first into the dirt. I jumped to my feet and delivered a fatal blow stabbing into his back.

I turned to face the giant I had knocked down who was now rushing at me head-on. Sidestepping his swing, I slashed him across the gut. He bent over from the blow momentarily and stopped mid-stride. He walked forward again as I brought the sword down across his lower back flinging him to the ground. My adrenaline was being pumped through my veins as I turned to face Glum's last foe. To my surprise, Glum had already beaten the beast down. I then turned to help Glam who managed to kill all his assailants. My body shook from the excessive adrenaline that coursed through it.

I had to find Sword no matter what the consequences. I called for Doc, and headed into the tundra without consulting Glum, or even considering what I was doing. All that mattered was locating Sword as quickly as possible. Doc came to my side and sensed the urgency of my needs.

Show me exactly where we were ambushed.
Follow me. It's not far.

Doc trotted into the brush and I kept pace. I

could not reach Sword fast enough. We traveled about two miles before Doc stopped.

This is the spot.

Help me find Sword.

I quickly looked around the small clearing and surrounding brush and found nothing, my search became more and more frantic. After a couple of hours of searching the same ground over and over I had an overwhelming feeling from deep inside that said I would not find it here. I raised my fists to the sky in defiance and screamed in anguish as loud as I could. I sensed Sword had been found by something other than the giants. It was imperative I find it fast! Without Sword all was lost, and I knew it.

Doc, can you find any fresh trails?

Doc sniffed the circumference of the area we had just searched before he signaled for me to come to where he was standing and told me about the fresh trail he had found. We both headed off after the quarry. We traversed the brush as fast as Doc could travel and still keep sight of the trail. A few hours later, Doc announced we were gaining on our prey. We followed the trail the rest of the day, and finally decided to rest once it became too dark to continue the chase.

Of course, we did not have the luxuries of Glum and his bag, but that seemed very trivial compared to finding Sword. I felt guilty for not telling Glum and Glam where I was going, but they would wait. I would not be able to rest until I found Sword. Doc and I cuddled up and I spent most of the night more restless than I had ever been. Finally, I drifted into an uneasy sleep.

I sat up to stare straight into the eyes of an ancient-looking man. He wore a magnificent crown encrusted with priceless jewels of every kind imaginable. He was dressed in a long white robe I would expect to be worn by angels, and he had a brilliant white aura around him. When he spoke, his voice commanded my attention, it was almost God like.

"Do not try to take the sword by force. Without it in your hands you do not stand a chance in battle against the ones who possess it."

"But how will I regain it then?"

"You will find a way. Just trust your instincts, they will not lead you astray. You must retrieve the Sword of Omens within forty hours or all is lost, and the Great Evil will once again be free."

"Who has Sword?"

"All I can tell you is that things may not be as they appear. I must leave now. Remember, trust your instincts and do not be fooled by your eyes."

The old man vanished. What did he mean by not being fooled by my eyes? I pondered his words and decided I would have to wait to find out. Dawn broke as the first of Surrea's two suns rose above the crest of the Valley of the Damned.

Since we had no breakfast or camp to break we simply began our quest for Sword. At first, Doc had a little trouble following the waning trail, but after a couple of hours we came across an abandoned camp site from last night. We now had a fresh trail to follow. They were only about half-an-hour in front of us now, and were heading out of the valley, traveling farther away from Dev'ilot.

It was imperative we recover Sword before they left the protective haze of the Valley of the Damned since Doc and I could not survive the frigid climate of the Hor'kuth Mountains clad as we were. Doc found five separate scents, four humanoid and one animal in the party. A few minutes later Doc announced they were just ahead of us. We had finally caught up to them!

Tom, something is strange. Two of them split off from the others. I believe they know we're following them. The two that split off are circling around and coming towards us from the left.

Stay out of sight Doc. Follow at a discrete distance. Stay just close enough to talk with me.

Doc disappeared into the brush. *Careful Tom, they are just behind and in front of you.*

I walked ten more steps, when a warrior barred the way in front of me. I was surrounded and knew the next few seconds were vital. Everything was at stake. The old man's words circled in my mind, without Sword I did not stand a chance in battle against these new foes.

"Why do you follow us warrior?" the fighter demanded.

I had to think quickly. Something told me they knew why I was here, so I tried to think of what a warrior from Surrea would say.

"Friend or foe?"

"That depends on why you are following us."

"I am looking for warriors brave enough to travel with me to Dev'ilot." What I said evidently struck a nerve, because his eyes grew wide with fear, and his whole attitude changed.

"Why would anyone want to go to such a place unless they were totally crazy or damned? Besides, Dev'ilot is just a legend, and I doubt it really exists."

"Do you not know where you are noble warrior?" I asked.

"No, pray tell us of our location."

"This is the Valley of the Damned. In the center of this valley is Niat'nuom Live, where Dev'ilot is supposed to be. There is a treasure there worth a king's ransom. I am after that treasure and cannot gain it alone. The Stone of Air is the biggest diamond in Surrea. I have been offered an enormous sum of money to recover the treasure." I took the chance that they were not only greedy, but stupid as well. "I alone know how to get in and out of the evil place without being detected." Might as well make it a good lie.

"Why do you lie, sir?"

The voice that accused me came from behind the one I had been talking with. The original speaker stepped aside and a large lion with wings came out from behind him to stand beside the fighter like a protector. Somehow the presence of the great beast put me at ease and I sensed it stood for all that was good. "What makes you think I lie?"

The fighter laughed. "This fool is not only ignorant, but stupid as well. Let's kill him and be done with it."

The warrior started to advance on me and I braced myself for a battle I already knew I could not win. Not without Sword. My mind raced. Something told me one of the five held Sword, and this would be my only chance to ever regain it. I had to pick the warrior who held Sword on the first try. If the one I picked did not have Sword all would be lost. Then I remembered what the old man in my vision said. "Things may not be as they appear." I was about to ask Doc if he had any idea which one possessed Sword when the winged lion came forward.

"Hold Or'lian. There is something strange here. The warrior is pure good, his aura is so pure I have never seen the like before. I am Larn'ish; evidently you are not familiar with the Larkian race. We are a noble race, lawful good in nature, and know when we are being lied to. I sense something strange about you. Please explain," the beast stated.

I felt I could not lie to the lion because it would know if I did. I had to come up with something quick. Considering it was a creature on the side of good, maybe I could reason with it, maybe telling it the truth would work. The old man told me to trust my instincts not my eyes and my instincts told me to trust the creature to do what was good for all that is good. Still, I felt caution was necessary since I really did not know who I was dealing with yet.

"Noble Larn'ish, I am the champion of good, it is true that part of what I said be false. But, on the other hand, part of what I said was true. This is the Valley of the Damned and Dev'ilot is in the center of it, and I am going there to find an item of great worth. Also, I could use help gaining it."

"But you are not going after a diamond, you have not been offered money to recover it, and you don't know how to get in or out of Dev'ilot. So, tell me what this great treasure is and your real reason for following us, because it sure was not to enlist our aid."

"That is true. Unfortunately, I was compelled to lie to you." I had to tell the real truth. "You possess something of mine, and I was not sure what type of essence your spirits contained. My name is Sterling the Great, I am after the Armor of Omens and you have my sword, the Sword of Kar'itma. The Sword of Omens! Without it *the one who cannot be named* will triumph and release the Great Evil from Dev'ilot and all that is good will cease to exist. I have no choice but to demand the sword, I must have it within the next few hours, and be on my way toward Dev'ilot."

I waited for a response to my words, but before the great beast could say anything, the warrior advanced to attack. The Larkian jumped in between the two of us and shouted at the fighter.

"Stop Or'lian! If you attack him you will have to fight me first. What he says is true."

"What!? You're taking sides with this fool?"

The lion growled. "Have you heard of the legend of the Battle of the Four Mages, Or'lian?"

"Yes, I've heard that old pixie tale."

"And you know what the final outcome is according to legend?"

"Yes, but no one believes such a sticktle story."

"The warrior that beat the Evil was Sterling the Great. He used the Items of Omens, this warrior has mentioned. He is either the great fighter of legend or truly believes he is. I recognize the shield he carries, it is the Shield of Omens and I already told you I thought that sword was the Sword of Omens. Either La'tian returns the weapon to its rightful owner, or I will take it!"

The fighter stood still with an unbelievable look of dismay etched across his stern features. We all stared at each other for the longest time, but nothing was stronger than the lion's dead stare.

Finally, the tense moment was broken and the warrior groaned. "La'tian, give the warrior his weapon and warrior take this rebel with you or I will kill him! Do not cross my path again Larn'ish or you will die!"

For the first time since I had set foot on Surrea I heard a female voice. It came from behind me and she had the sweetest musical tone I had ever heard.

"Here warrior."

I turned to see what kind of creature made such an engaging sound and came face to face with the most gorgeous woman I had ever seen. My eyes were captivated by her deep rich tan that highlighted the long golden hair which caressed her back. She was pretty much clad in the same fashion that Glam was and her eyes, one blue, the other green, were the deepest in color imaginable. Her features were perfect in every way. Mesmerized by those magnificent eyes, I became transfixed in a hypnotic state unable to move or talk and she seemed to be in the same state.

We stood there for I don't know how long staring into each other's eyes. She had Sword in her hand and was ready to deliver it to mine while my outstretched hand was so close to the hilt I could almost feel it. I was so bewitched by her beauty I failed to grasp the item I held so highly precious. Finally snapping back to reality, I tenderly took my weapon from her soft grasp giving a courteous nod, and a squeaky thank you which she returned the gesture with a crackled, your welcome.

She nodded and smiled at me. I had heard of love at first sight, but never really believed it was possible, that is till now. I sensed this beautiful woman was experiencing the same feelings. Sword exchanged hands while our unblinking gaze never broke. Then as one we quit looking into each other's eyes. She looked toward the fighter and the great beast, while I could not take my eyes off of the most perfect female body I had ever seen, taking in every inch of it from head to toe.

"Larn'ish, if you and this noble fighter do not mind, I would like to accompany you on your quest."

"What is going on here?" Or'lian asked. "Does anyone else want to rebel against me? Who is this human that follows us and then demands from us, next to steal my friends from me? Do I have to kill him to keep the rest of you from falling prey to his spell?"

"Or'lian, do you not understand? He is the champion for the side of all that is good; his destiny is to fight the champion of evil. If he fails, evil will destroy everything that is good. That means us! It means every race on Surrea except the evil ones. You profess to belong to the neutral alignments, which would also be destroyed. If the legend is true, this human is the best warrior in existence, without doubt. He could have taken the sword by force if he wanted to."

"I am familiar with these tales, but do they not also mention a companion? A great wolf I believe, if this is truly the champion of legend, where is his beast?"

There was a very sarcastic sting to his voice, but before I could defend myself, Doc proudly walked over to my side and raised his head to stand as tall as he possibly could. I did not think of him as a wolf, or a beast. Just my best friend, good old Doc.

This should shut up the big oaf. I sensed he was about to attack, but he just now thought better of it.

The fighter seemed completely stifled by Doc's appearance. He lowered his sword and backed up.

"La'tian I believe it was? I would be honored to have you join us."

Doc and I, with our two new companions split off from the other three, two of which I never saw and headed toward our final destination.

CHAPTER ELEVEN

Niat'nuom Live

There was no time to backtrack to find Glum and Glam even though I felt we would probably need them. Some choices were not ours to make, so I led the group straight for Niat'nuom Live.

An unusual name for a mountain in the middle of a valley referred to as the Valley of the Dead. The mountain was a volcano so it did seem appropriate after all. Of course, live was evil, and Niat'nuom was mountain if you spelled them both backwards. Evil Mountain definitely fit the wicked volcano better than its given name. I wondered if there was any significance to it being spelled in reverse?

We exchanged stories while we walked and quickly became friends. I had great difficulty keeping my mind on the mission and off the shapely figure of the gorgeous woman that fate brought to me. Deep down I feared she could endanger my mission. Could my feelings for this beauty get in the way of success? There was always the chance I would have to decide between her life and victory. I tried not to think about it.

Every time I glanced at her, she was looking longingly at me. I wanted her. I had to get that thought out of my mind, but with every step I took my desire grew. The harder I tried, the more I failed. All I could think about was being close to that gorgeous body.

"So, you're the warrior of legends. I never dreamed the greatest warrior in the universe would be so handsome."

"I have seen many fascinating and beautiful sights, but all of them seem ugly in comparison to your stunning beauty." She blushed and then giggled. Her eyes told me what I really wanted to know.

She looked deep into my eyes. "Sterling, I desire you greatly."

I felt my entire being melt at those wonderful words. Suddenly I felt like a boy again on his first date. Then Doc growled.

Sorry to butt in Tom, but there's something following us.

"Sterling, we are being followed!" Larn'ish stated just a split second after Doc did.

"Larn'ish, La'tian continue on, Doc follow me." I started to circle around. *Doc let me know when they've passed us.*

They're animals, and there's three of them. Doc stood watch. *They've passed. But Tom, I must warn you, they're flesh eaters looking for a meal.*

Back me up, I'm going in from behind. I rose up from our hiding place and jumped into the middle of a clearing and found myself in the midst of three saber-toothed tigers the size of small horse**s**. I froze in amazement. How do you fight three large tigers with a sword and shield? I had no time to ponder the answer because the closest tiger reacted to my presence and leapt into the air straight at me.

I lifted my shield just in time to reflect one of the beast's front paws, but the claws on the other foot ripped through my sword arm and delivered a deep, long gash. I dropped Sword and pain shot through me. The beast landed on its side with a loud thud and I dropped to my knees to try and retrieve Sword. Great, I had no plan, was severely wounded, and the tigers did not even have a scratch.

I pushed my pain aside, grabbed Sword, and rolled to avoid a well-aimed swipe at my head. The giant cat that landed close to me just stared with deadly eyes. I panicked since I could not see a way out. The prehistoric animal leapt into the air and was about to land on me. My shield was pinned between my body and a tree, and Sword was underneath me. I had no weapon or protection, no way to defend myself. The large cat charged at me with blinding speed, more than capable of delivering death with a single blow. Is this how my journey would end? I was paralyzed with fear.

The tiger flew through the air and I felt like I was watching a movie in slow motion. All I saw was those four-inch claws protruding from its paws aimed at my head. To my surprise it moved in a tangent from its original course and I realized my life had been saved by the Larkian. Quickly regaining my feet, I saw the other two tigers fighting each other and Larn'ish was embroiled in a vicious and bloody fight with the third one.

Since Larn'ish saved my life I felt I owed him the same in return. The giant tiger had my winged comrade down and was tearing him apart. I ran to his aid and sliced the hind quarters of the great beast. It let out a deafening roar, turned and took a swipe at me. I blocked the attack with Sword and sliced through its limb. When the animal started to rise, I took advantage of his precarious position and buried Sword into his skull. He growled, shivered and then laid still on top of Larn'ish.

The other two animals still fought each other. Bewildered by what had transpired so far, I stood transfixed watching the great struggle going on before me. Both cats were severely wounded until one finally ended up on top of the other holding his opponent by the throat in a death grip.

Thinking this was a perfect opportunity to kill two birds with one stone, I ran up and brought Sword down into the back of the neck of the cat that had gained victory over its fallen prey. His neck snapped when Sword easily clove through the thick muscles and buried itself in the other beast's upper spine. Both bodies stiffened then went limp.

My new-found companion was still buried beneath the hulking mass of the dead sabretooth. I tried to move the huge limp body, but could not even budge it. "La'tian, come quickly!" I hoped her added strength might enable me to remove the enormous weight from our friend.

The great lion gasped. "It is no use, Sterling, I am finished, I have fulfilled my gleaus."

Those were his last words as his lungs filled with air one more time and his final breath left his body. La'tian was now at my side, and I saw the sun glisten off the wet streak on her cheek where the tears she has had shed left a watery trail.

"What did he mean by I have fulfilled my gleaus?"

"The Larkians are a good and noble race, they believe they are born to fulfill their own personal final destiny. Evidently saving your life was his. But you are hurt; let me see your wound."

La'tian's words hit home like a sudden migraine, I had completely forgotten the large gash in my forearm. It was bleeding profusely, and now that the adrenalin had slowed, the pain welled up like a volcano ready to blow. The beautiful warrior dressed my wound, her touch soft and elegant. She seemed like a very experienced nurse, one I would welcome no matter what condition I was in.

Before she finished wrapping my arm, her body pressed against mine and she became too irresistible to resist. I grabbed her and kissed her long and hard. Our embrace grew tighter and our kiss became deeper. Then Doc growled.

Uh hum, we do have a purpose for being here, Tom.

Doc, your timing really sucks.

So does fighting giant cats, but we do what we have to do.

You're too bossy for a dog. I gently ended the

kiss and pulled back.

"Is something wrong? Did I not please you?"

"Quite the contrary, my love. But before we get lost in each other, we have a universe to save." If she only knew how hard that was to say. I must have gone completely insane because all I could think about now was my destiny. This was turning out the way Asmond said it would. Since this gorgeous lady came into my life, I now had something to fight for.

After burying the Larkian, we left our feelings behind and continued on toward Dev'ilot. I was finally at peace with myself, and I could taste success for the first time in this long and arduous quest. Yet I still felt like good old Thomas Brown, not Sterling the Great, and somehow was troubled by this.

Doc, La'tian and I marched towards an uncertain fate, but still managed to keep our spirits high despite the loss of our winged friend. The terrain had been approximately the same since the day we had entered the Valley of the Damned, until hours after our encounter with the saber-toothed tigers. Now it began to resemble the La Brea Tar Pits in Los Angeles, California.

An extremely putrid smell floated in the air, along with the smell of death. The heat had become unbearable and I finally removed my torn and tattered shirt, which gave no relief from the blistering heat. Doc panted heavily in an effort to lower his body temperature, but there was no escape. The closer we came to Dev'ilot, the more miserable the climate and terrain became.

The tar pits gave way to pits of bubbling lava that put a heavy layer of sulfur into the air. If it got much worse we would all be dead. There was not one living plant or animal around due to the extreme heat and intolerable air. I took a few more steps when La'tian collapsed from the unbearable climate. I sheathed Sword and had to pick her up and put her over my shoulder in a fireman's carry,

Doc and I struggled on, careful not to fall into one of the lava pools. Back and forth we walked. It seemed like we were going in circles to avoid lava. I calculated we were about a mile from Niat'nuom Live. I had trouble breathing and feared Doc could not take another step. I bent down to check him and found the pads of his feet were starting to show signs of being burnt by the surface we were traveling on, which was not surprising since I felt considerable heat through my thick boots.

I strapped the shield onto my back and put him over my shoulder. I called on every ounce of reserves I had left to continue on. I wondered how far I would make it with the added weight, not to mention the extra heat from their bodies. I stumbled on in a daze and refused to stop. I had to make it to that mountain, no matter what the consequences might be. I fought with each step to go on, and with each step it grew more difficult and I wondered if I could take another.

The good news was the mountain was now less than half a mile. I knit my brow with determination and in two hours I stood at the base of the live volcano. I lowered Doc to the ground, then carefully laid La'tian down. Fighting the blackness that tried to engulf my conscious spirit, I searched the surrounding countryside for some sort of shelter from the blistering heat.

I thought I saw a cave off to my left and decided to investigate, feeling Doc and La'tian would be safe here for the short time it would take me to check it out. The moment I took my first step, the rocky terrain beneath my feet began to shake and swell. I stumbled forward as the ground opened underneath me and I fell about twenty feet before I hit bottom. My head bounced off the rock floor so hard everything went black.

When I opened my eyes, I had no idea how long I had been out. My shield ended up on top of me and Sword was beside me. I tried to get up, but found my left arm hurt so bad it had to be broken and I could barely move my fingers. I rose slowly to my feet and realized my arm was not the only casualty.

Every muscle and bone in my body screamed painfully. Soon my strength returned and breathing was normal, even though the cave was extremely hot. This heat was easier to breathe than on the surface. My arm had slowly come back to life, and apparently was not broken, but still hurt to the point it was difficult to hold my shield. But hold it I did, since every place I had traveled to on this planet had been hostile so far and I doubted this cave would be any different.

I looked around and found I was in a wondrous cave lined with an unusual illuminated growth that kept changing the color of light it gave off. These plants grew in large sporadic patches and provided ample light to see by. The cave looked like a dead cave. Except for the strange fungus, only stalagmites and stalactites could be seen. I wandered down the rock corridor and looked for a way back to the surface.

Hours passed while I wandered down one corridor after another. It was a natural maze, yet somehow, I felt I knew exactly where I was going. I gave up finding a way to the surface because I doubted I could locate the place where I left my friends. I began to feel a deep depression slowly creep into my soul from having the unmistakable feeling that my best friend and the new love of my life were no more.

Knowing that I was now alone to tackle whatever laid before me only added to this feeling. I could only pray my two friends survived, but somehow, I knew they were dead and felt it was my fault for not carrying them a few more steps. I could have saved their lives! I failed them. Sorrow filled my heart for the loss of my best friend and the love I had just found. Bitterness welled up inside me knowing I would never be able to experience the love I needed so badly. A hate I never felt before reared its ugly head, and I wished I had an enemy to take my frustration out on, something to kill! I got my wish.

I walked along in a daze. All my thoughts were on Doc and La'tian. What I should have done, what I wanted to do. Would those thoughts ever stop? Then a spear came out of nowhere, and by pure chance hit my shield. That snapped me out of my day dream and back to the situation at hand. The spear rebounded and disappeared into the cave's depths on my left, and a piercing scream let me know it found its owner.

While I raced toward the area the spear came from, my anger caused me to run recklessly head-on toward an unknown assailant. By pure luck my stupid reaction might have saved my life. A dozen more spears landed harmlessly where I had just stood. I ran and more spears flew by, luckily none found their mark. It was then I remembered the saying, "be careful what you wish for." That made me smile.

Whenever possible I deflected spears with my shield and was rewarded by a scream of agony. I ran full speed in the direction the first spear came from, and it was a considerable distance. That's when I realized something was astray. There were no creatures, no spears, and no bodies.

Who threw the spears? I was in a large cavern and came to a wall. Still no creatures, but spears continued to rain down around me. If I stopped I would become an easy target, so I followed the wall at a good run. The farther I traveled in the large cavern the darker it became. The area was barely lit by the fungus and I could hardly see a few feet in front of me. Finally, I came to an off-shoot tunnel and immediately turned into it.

The moment I entered the corridor the spears ceased to fall around me. I ran about twenty feet and abruptly came to a dead end. I heard the sounds of leathery feet approaching from the entrance of the tomb I had selected. I stood ready for combat. Most of the anger I felt had been replaced by the common sense of knowing I was alone and if I was going to live through this I had to remain level headed. However, I was still worked up enough to take my wrath out on the poor creatures that dared challenge me. "Come on you slimy cave dwellers! Who wants to be the first to die at the hands of Sterling the Great?" I waited to see what type of creature would enter the dim light.

All I saw were the shadows of humanoid figures about five feet tall. The shadows took shape while they ran toward me. Finally, I saw my adversaries clearly. They looked like a cross between a lizard and a man. They stood erect with the body of a humanoid, the head and tail of a lizard, and webbed hands and feet. To make things worse, they were completely covered with scales like a fish. And they topped off their appearance with fur pelts.

As they approached, the two in front threw their spears. I used my shield to deflect the spears and they flew past their shoulders as they ran toward me, but I was still rewarded by a shriek behind them. They continued to come at me and the ones behind them must have given up throwing their spears at me, deciding hand to hand combat was a better idea because they made gurgling noises and charged. I had no idea how many of these lizard things there were, so I decided to fight easy in an effort to conserve my energy. I had to survive.

The first one reached me and I easily cut him down, two more swipes and another two dead. These guys were easy prey and I threw caution to the wind. Maybe if I charged them and quickly cut down a few more they might decide there was easier prey elsewhere.

The wind suddenly picked up while I tried my maneuver. To my surprise the lizard things' eyes grew wide with fear, some pointed in my direction, and one even dropped his spear. They all turned and ran recklessly away from my onslaught. That is when I heard a deep laugh behind me.

CHAPTER TWELVE

The Last Challenge

I turned and came face to face with the creature from my very first dream on the night I found the ring. A giant lizard with wings, a dragon, only that one was white, this one is golden. Dreams sometimes do come true whether you want them to or not.

"Ah, dinner! If I know your name you will taste better!" it bellowed, followed by another deep laugh.

The sound of its laugh made my skin crawl. "I don't suppose you would settle for these dead lizard creatures?" I pointed at the bodies that littered the cavern floor. I hoped to change his mind about tonight's dinner menu. I was no match for this beast, and if the legends on earth came from facts on Surrea about dragons, he could breathe fire so I could not out run the beast.

"I plan on eating them first, and then you for desert. Lizardmen are stringy and tough, but humans are a delicacy I have not tasted for quite some time. Since you refuse to tell me your name you must evidently be ashamed of it. No matter. Prepare to die at the hands of Omens the Great and Powerful!"

The name shocked me, could there be a connection between the items I possessed and this frightening creature? I stood straight and tall and in a last act of defiance yelled, "I am Sterling the Great, and I possess three of the items of Omens. If I have to kill you mighty Omens the Great and Powerful to continue my destiny, so be it!"

The dragon's features changed, and so did his tone.

"The time of the *one that cannot be named* is at hand, my destiny is finally coming to an end. Great Sterling, I have waited here seven hundred and eighty-nine years for your return. The ring has brought you here to me; only through me can you fulfill your own destiny. I am the beginning and the end. Before you can gain the last item, you must go through one last challenge."

The dragon scooped up a dead lizardman with his mouth and proceeded to eat it. I heard a sickening crunching sound while the terrifying creature chewed its meal. I waited impatiently because I had to, but time was running out.

"I was given the responsibility of guarding the holding place of the last item, along with the knowledge of gaining the one key. Long ago I was handed this onus, and I have been waiting for your return great warrior. At last, my destiny is about to be fulfilled. Enter the portal, do not return until you have found the key of Draxstill, you will find it in the Plains of Dar'moun. Once you gain the key, return to the portal and enter it. I warn you, do not enter the portal without the key. Once you are back here, the key will lead you to the Armor of Kim'imota. One last thing, you will only have ten hours before your air runs out."

He led me to a shimmering black portal that was suspended in mid-air just above the floor and wished me good luck. As I stepped into it, I wondered what he meant about my air running out? It was like stepping through a doorway, I found myself on the floor of a massive body of water that had to be an ocean or a large lake and I was surrounded by an air bubble.

When I was free of the portal, I turned and saw the same *black hole* the dragon led me to. My way back. I walked around the portal out of curiosity, but when I came around the side of it, there seemed to be no depth to the object and it disappeared, only visible from the front. Great, I thought, that should make it really easy to find again. Like I really needed to add to my problems. I checked my watch since the dragon warned me about my air supply. Surprisingly my timepiece still worked. It was a miracle considering what I had been through. Thinking I should do a commercial for the maker when I got home. So, I picked a direction and ran at the normal speed the boots allowed. It was like I was running on land, not inside a bubble underwater because there was no drag. This was one bubble I did not want to burst.

I continued at a full run toward an unknown destination and passed one unique and fantastic sight after another. Under different circumstances, I would have enjoyed spending the whole day examining every sight in minute detail. I saw so many exotic plants and fish but could only admire them for a split second while I raced by.

The Plains of Dar'moun that Omens spoke of was first on my list. Of course, I had no idea where this place was, but I would find it. The ring brought me this far and I knew in my heart that it would never let me down.

I ran for a while admiring the beauty of the watery depths, when by complete surprise I was caught up in a large net of wrought-iron metal. It must have been hidden under the top layer of sand in the watery waste. It completely entrapped me. It even entered my air bubble and made it virtually impossible for me to move. There was no means of escape. Just as soon as I was trapped, several monsters that looked like the *Creature from the Black Lagoon* appeared from nowhere.

They were completely hairless and covered with greenish-orange scales instead of skin. Their hands and feet were webbed and their heads resembled the head of a catfish. I felt trapped, at the mercy of these aquatic creatures. They made some gurgling noises to each other and looked to be arguing with one another.

They are called mermen. They will have to take you to their king before they can decide what to do with you. Unfortunately, they hate all land dwellers and will probably kill you. We must find a means of escape. Sword stated.

The mermen must have finally ended their long argument because they quit talking among themselves. One of them blew a long blast on a large seashell which made a loud, low octave tone. A few seconds later an extremely large crab-like creature strode toward me through the murky depths. One of the mermen mounted the crab, shouted what seemed to be orders to the beast, which in turn grabbed the net surrounding me and lifted me off the sandy floor. Within seconds we were off toward and unknown destination.

After the strange little party had marched for about half an hour, we came to a giant clam that was the size of a small house. A merman blew another blast on his seashell, and the giant clam opened its shell to show its vulnerable self to the outside world. The merman promptly threw me into the monstrous clam which closed around me.

I had no idea how long I laid entangled in that desolate absolute darkness, but finally my living prison opened to relinquish its prisoner. I found myself in a large chamber that must be the throne room in this underwater kingdom. My living prison was just a couple of feet from a set of twelve steps that led up to a large throne made entirely out of shells. Perched upon this throne was a very large merman adorned with all sorts of shells and precious gems, and he had a golden crown on top of his head.

The chamber was filled with at least a couple-hundred mermen from what appeared to be all sorts of social ranks. What caught my eye was a mermaid chained by the neck to the king's throne. The king gurgled commands and the mermaid responded to them.

"The Great King Longfin wishes to know your name and rank, land dweller."

"Tell his highness my name is Sterling the Great, I am the champion of all that is good."

The mermaid's eyes lit up when I mentioned my name, and she quickly relayed the information. The entire assembly laughed, including the king. He once again garbled some more commands to his beautiful interpreter.

"The Great King Longfin will graciously allow you to prove yourself great warrior. I have heard of you, but alas even the Great Sterling cannot stand up to the monstrous Draxstill. He…" She started to say, but the king made a sharp hard tug on her chain stopping the rest of her sentence.

"Why does he wish me to kill this Draxstill?"

The mermaid once again conveyed my words, and once again the throng burst out in laughter. The king laughed so hard he could barely speak and took several minutes before he could deliver commands to the mermaid.

"Draxstill is their god, but he is an evil and dangerous monster. He makes lots of demands from the Dark Pool Clan, and they would love to see him destroyed. Many have tried, all have failed. If you succeed in destroying the beast, the Great King Longfin will grant you two wishes and let you leave in peace. But I warn you warrior, as soon as they let you loose in the Plains of Dar'moun, avoid the beast and try to escape. You are no match for the monster."

"It is my destiny to find the Key of Draxstill. Do you know where it is located?"

"Then you are already dead, for the Key of Draxstill is around Draxstill's neck, the only way to gain this key is to destroy the evil thing," the mermaid answered.

"Tell the king I am ready to accept the challenge."

No sooner than the mermaid told the king my answer, he gurgled and waived his webbed hand. Two guards came over and took the net off of me, and I was once again engulfed by darkness when the giant clam shut its shell. Roughly thirty minutes later, the clam released me, and the moment I climbed out the clam swam away. I was once again alone in the murky depths, ready to discover the intricacies of this new challenge.

My air bubble had diminished in size which obviously indicated I was running out of air. I had no time to spare so I yelled out my enemy's name and was quickly answered by a muffled growl in the near distance.

At first, I only saw the shadowed outline of a creature not yet in my view. It moved quickly and I now faced a creature the size of one of the stone giants. Its features were completely hidden by the seaweed that covered its entire body. The only part of him not hidden were two glowing yellow eyes with a demonic glint to them. Otherwise it looked humanoid, standing on two legs and having two arms.

"I have come for the key of Draxstill." I took a deep breath to maintain my confidence. "Either you can give it to me and go in peace, or I will kill you and take it."

"No one has ever fought with Draxstill and lived, little Sterling. That's right, I know your name dackle of good. You cannot win against me, my master has influenced the realm of space and time causing a rift, and this rift he caused was in my favor. I am your downfall little human. It is you who is going to die!"

"You cannot win, evil one. There is something you are not aware of, something only I and one other knows. I have been given the edge to counteract your master's meddling mischief," I said as the behemoth approached, trying to put the slightest doubt into its mind.

He abruptly came at me with startling speed. I braced myself for his attack, not knowing what to expect.

Draxstill came within fifteen feet of me, stopped and raised a seaweed-covered arm which he pointed at me. His action bothered me, as well it should have. A dozen strands of seaweed came out of his outstretched arm; these strands flew through the water like arrows towards me. I crouched behind my shield and reflected seven of the twelve strands. Two strands wrapped around one leg and two around my other leg, the fifth went over my shield, curved and wrapped around an arm. All five seaweeds bit into my skin and caused searing pain. I looked up to see the seven I had reflected circle around and come back toward me, followed by another dozen from Draxstill's other arm.

There was no way I could fight these things all at once, so I started to run, but the four around my legs had intertwined with each other and made it impossible for me to move. I took a quick slice at them between my legs. They squealed when Sword cut through them. They wiggled in agony and fell off my legs. The strands were evidently living creatures, possibly acting separately from their host Draxstill.

I turned and ran from the nineteen strands that flew through the water toward me, tearing at the fifth strand that attached itself to my arm. I sliced it in half and was shocked that when the thing squealed it opened a mouth complete with teeth, and it had eyes that looked at me before it fell to its death. I was covered with my own blood. Even though their teeth were small, they were razor sharp causing wounds that were not deep but still bled profusely like a nick from shaving.

The sandy floor was level in all directions, so I turned and ran backwards, slicing at the strands before they grabbed me. Of the nineteen, only two made it through Sword's flashing movements. One attached itself to my sword arm, the other wrapped around my waist. I quickly dispatched those two before they could cut me. I could not afford to lose any more blood.

"You have to do better than that, Draxstill. Your little friends are no match for the Sword of Omens."

"Maybe the eelweeds are not, but a crablord will be!"

He threw a dozen more of the nasties at me. That put the count at thirty-six eelweeds he had tossed my way and unless my eyes were playing tricks on me, Draxstill had shrunk a good two or three feet in height. I turned to run, using the same tactic that had worked so well on the last bunch of eelweeds, and found myself staring straight at one of the giant crabs I had seen earlier under the mermen's control. The crab advanced at me with several eelweeds coming from behind. I had to make a quick decision and hope it was the right one.

I had seen these giant crabs move, and they seemed to be slow and sluggish, so I decided to run around it, take out the eelweeds and then deal with the crab. I turned to my right and found six more of the eelweeds coming at me. With no time to waste I charged into them slicing and blocking what I could to stay free of the creatures.

I chopped three down, blocked two more, but the sixth managed to wrap itself around my leg. I ran around the crab to put a little distance between us, pulled the eelweed off my leg before it could trip me up and dispatched it to its private hell. When I turned to face the horde of eelweeds rushing toward me something was missing from the scene in front of me, but I couldn't place it. I ran backwards chopping every eelweed I could reach. Something clubbed me hard from behind. I flew through the murky waters and landed on my back with eleven remaining eelweeds in hot pursuit.

The blow knocked me silly, but I forced myself to my feet. The little creatures were almost on me, but when I turned to run, a huge claw came at my head. I ducked just in time to miss the crab's pincher and I heard a snap where my neck had been. Now I realized what had been missing from the scene, the crab should have been there, but somehow it must have maneuvered around me and hit me from behind. I heard Draxstill's laugh off to my left and decided to go to the right. I needed to take care of his minions before I could deal with him.

I ran around the crab, turned and started chopping the eelweeds that had overtaken me. Once again, the crab was nowhere in sight and I was not going to be taken advantage of again. I switched direction to the left and caught the crab out of the corner of my eye. After I sliced the last eelweed, I turned and faced the crablord. At first it was right in front of me, the next second it was gone, it just vanished.

I spun around to locate the thing, and by pure chance blocked its claw with my shield. The accidental maneuver I pulled, threw it off balance and I took full advantage of the situation. I stepped forward and cut through one of its legs. The crablord squealed and took a swing at me with its other claw. I sidestepped then brought Sword down to completely sever the appendage. I twisted and rammed Sword into its shell. It lurched up, rolled over and went stiff.

I turned and stared at Draxstill. "Don't send a crab to do a Draxstill's job!"

"What's the matter human? You seem to be losing quite a bit of blood. Maybe a couple more crablords will help?" He tossed another bunch of eelweeds at me.

I was fed up with dealing with all the creepy creatures. It was about time I dealt with the main problem, Draxstill. It did not matter if the crablord had the ability to disappear and reappear at will, I planned to take him on and win. I put my trusty boots into high gear and charged straight for my goal, slowing enough to cut down the eelweeds between him and me. It was apparent my foe had steadily shrunk in size. He began at around eighteen feet tall and was now down to about twelve. The closer I came to him the more the seaweed he was covered with seemed to be alive, but of course they were actually eelweeds.

I was fifteen feet from him when two crablords appeared out of nowhere and blocked my way. I felt two crablords, more eelweeds and Draxstill might be more than I could handle all at once, so I figured it might be to my benefit to even the odds a little. I ran straight for one of the overgrown crustaceans, dodged its claws, rolled underneath it and stabbed straight up into the center of the thing. Evidently it did not care much for the taste of cold steel, because it screeched, rolled over and died. I jumped up as the crab lurched up from Sword's bitter bite, the second crablord advanced on me.

I jumped toward Draxstill, who was now only six feet from me, severing the crablord's claw when it tried to stop my advance. I blocked Draxstill's fist when it came at me with incredible speed, then swung through his midsection, slicing Sword completely through him. I heard several separate squeals, and half a dozen or so eelweeds fell to the ground dead, yet Draxstill was not affected by the blow.

The shock of seeing him withstand a sword pass through his body without even fazing him caught me off guard, and so did the crablord. Its pincher clasped me around my waist, and I felt my life force being cut in half, along with my body. I took a desperate blind swing behind me, which proved my luck was strong, because Sword hit home severing the appendage from its host's body, thus releasing me from the death grip. The crablord was now harmless, allowing me to turn my full attention toward Draxstill.

He would probably summon several more crablords to his aid. I did not want to give him a chance. I advanced on him and started swinging wildly. One stroke after another sliced through his body, eelweeds fell to the ground like flies on a hot summer day around a bug zapper. Draxstill had diminished in size with each swing until finally a blow caused him to explode. The remaining eelweeds flew in all directions, several of which attached to me. When they were all gone the only thing left was the skeleton of some unknown creature that simply collapsed to the ground in a small pile.

The eelweeds that were attached to me also fell. When I looked down at the scattered bones lying at my feet I spotted a golden chain and picked it up. At the end of this chain was a triple pronged metallic item, the Key of Draxstill.

Not knowing which direction to go, I simply ran in the direction I was pointed. My air bubble had diminished to a tenth of its original size and was shrinking at an accelerated rate. I urgently needed to find the portal. I hastened my speed, but it was a losing battle. I had been running for over ten minutes when I spotted an underwater city a short distance ahead. I started running as fast as I could but felt there was no way I could find the portal by myself. Even with the ring's guidance I did not have the time. My only hope was the mermen and their king's promise to me. Either the city in front of me was theirs, or it would be my watery grave.

When I was close to the city's gates, two guards advanced toward me on crablords. I could not out-maneuver the giant crab's unique ability, so I let them take me. For some reason I lifted the Key of Draxstill for them to see. Evidently they recognized it, because they became very excited and motioned for me to climb aboard their mounts. I even think they argued over who would have the honor of escorting me. I was in no position to waste time so I jumped up on the nearest crab.

The one I picked had a huge grin on his face, and the other wore a large frown which just convinced me all the more that my hunch was correct. I motioned for my chauffeur to hurry, and the next thing I knew I was in the throne room. The king still sat in the same position he had been in when I departed. His eyes lit up when he saw me, then a look of anger crossed his face. He gurgled loudly and waved his arms wildly as if in a rage.

"The Great King Longfin wishes to know why you have returned without finishing the challenge you accepted?"

Longfin's interpreter's voice was soothing, and

she was extremely beautiful. I had no time for distractions, nor was I in the mood since I had just lost the woman I had fallen in love with. "Tell the king I have defeated Draxstill and have brought proof of my victory." I brought the key out from behind my shield where I hid it for all to see. A hush fell over the entire assembly. The king's look of anger turned to one of disbelief and then joy. Finally, the king raved insanely and practically jumped up and down in a fit of happiness and joy, broke the silence. The only two living things in the entire hall other than me that did not go into a raving fit was the mermaid and the crab I was perched on.

"The Great King Longfin thanks the Great Warrior Sterling for saving his people from the intolerable suffering Draxstill inflicted upon them. He will now grant you the wishes promised and then allow you to go in peace. You have become like a god unto these people, Sterling. Use this to your advantage; but I warn you, do not trust them. They also want the key and will kill you to get it."

"Can you control this crablord, mermaid?"

"Yes, but as you can see I am enslaved."

"Tell the king I want a banquet in my honor and a slave of my choosing, in those exact words."

The mermaid conveyed my demands, and I could tell by his reactions he accepted, but I would still wait for the beautiful mermaid to tell me.

"He graciously accepts your requests and says he has an entire kingdom from which to pick your slave. He also wants the key."

"Tell him I will give him the key at the banquet;

also tell him I have already picked my slave. What is your name, anyway?"

"De'larla."

"Well De'larla, as soon as I cut your chain, mount this crab and get us out of here, can you do that?"

"Yes, as long as the merman beside you is not on it."

"Don't worry about him, I will take care of that. Now tell the king what I said, and we will see what happens."

I hopped down from my ride and began to head toward my only hope of making it to the portal in time. My air bubble was close to gone. The moment I neared the chain, the mermaid spoke.

"He wants the key now."

I cut the chain with one blow, sparks flew as Sword severed it and cut a deep gash in the rock floor.

"Tell him not to question my kindness, I have powers he does not understand, and could easily destroy his kingdom if I so desired. Tell him, his minions did not capture me, but that I allowed them to and could have killed him the first time we met. The only reason I didn't, was because I may have need of him and his followers in the future. If he does not like my mercy, then I will kill everyone in this room, starting with him. Say it as if I scared you, do you understand? Say it loud enough for all to hear."

I grabbed the four-foot of chain that was still attached to the mermaid's neck and dragged her back toward the crablord. While she spoke my words to the assembly, I did not look back to see how he responded to my defiance, but the faces of the mermen I saw appeared to be in shock. I jumped aboard the crablord and waited for the mermaid to finish her translation. When she was done there was a long pause in the room. It became so quiet you could have heard a pin drift to the stone floor. "Tell him, I have been angered and will not give him the key. I am leaving, whether he likes it or not, and will decide later if I will return with it. And, I will kill anyone who gets in my way!"

She gave my newest statements to his royal highness, and as soon as I could tell she had finished, I swung at the guard sitting on the crab beside me. The guard's head went flying through the water, signifying I meant business. The entire room was aghast at my actions, the king went hysterical and shouted at his mermen who spurred into action.

"They're attacking!" The mermaid mounted the crab.

"Get us out of here, now!" I put my arm around her waist and the throne room disappeared, quickly replaced by the familiar waters I had grown accustomed to. "Do you know where the portal is?"

The pressure of the ocean's depth that the air bubble protected me from began to be apparent to my unprotected skin. I used the last of my precious air to describe the portal to her. If she was unfamiliar with my only means of escape, this place would become my watery grave. I could no longer see any air between me and the murky depths, but I was still dry so evidently, I still had one or two breaths left before my air supply was completely exhausted. My vision blurred and I could no longer focus to the point I was virtually blinded. I gasped for breath. All hope was gone. My journey would end here. The Great Evil had won.

I took my last breath and at the very end of it took in a little water. The full pressure of the oceans depths hit me all at once, knocking the last bit of air I tried to cling to from my lungs. I thought I felt something gently pick me up as I fell toward an unconscious state.

CHAPTER THIRTEEN

Two's Company and Three Are Dead

My hands felt dry rock and my lungs filled with fresh air. I gasped in pain. Every little cut on my body burned from the salt water that had finally reached my skin. I was soaked, sore and worn out, when I heard an unfamiliar voice with a very evil tone to it.

"The human sticktle actually succeeded in defeating the weakling Draxstill."

"Or ran in disgrace!"

Three or four separate laughs made me cringe. I blinked several times to focus on the strangers.

"Well, let's complete our mission and return with his head to Sar'garian."

My head instantly cleared when I heard that name. I needed the element of surprise if I was going to gain the upper hand with these creatures who planned to kill me. I remembered a dream I had in the Tre'ton's home, *the one that cannot be named* had sent five of his best to keep me from gaining the last item. I would have made a large wager I was lying on the ground in front of them.

Heavy footsteps came closer to me and I waited until the last second and flipped over as I heard his weapon whistle through the air. I blocked the large two-handed bastard sword with my shield and swung with all my might at his knees. Sword sliced clean through his armor and both legs, severing them just below the kneecaps. His sword rebounded and threw him backwards. He screamed in sheer agony and fell at the feet of his companions. The warrior wriggled in extreme pain as his life's blood spurted into the air and onto the ground from the fatal wounds where his legs should have been. The severed legs stood in their animal-hide boots as if supporting some unseen creature for a second before they tipped over, twitching in a spasmodic dance of death.

I jumped up ready for the next one's advancement and wondered what had happened to the Golden Dragon. I did not have to contemplate on Omens' whereabouts for long. Behind the three warriors standing before me was Omens' decapitated body, and to their left were the charred remains of what I guessed to be the fifth member of this unholy group.

"Who is next to die at the hands of Sterling the Great? Three to one. You'd better get reinforcements scum bags, you're slightly outnumbered!" Adrenaline coursed through my veins as I faced two fully armored fighters and a human dressed like a monk who immediately spurred into action. The one in the middle had a shield shaped like a heart, with the design of a black dragon painted on it. He held a metallic whip and wore a bright red cape that covered his jet-black armor. He grabbed the cape, wrapped it around himself and vanished into thin air.

I backed up against the wall just in case he had abilities similar to a crablord. I did not want him to attack me from behind. The one on the right carried a diamond shaped shield painted blood red with no design, had a battle-axe and also wore jet-black armor. The last wore only a robe and had no visible shield; he held only a long bow, which he promptly shot at me. The one with the battle-axe gave a battle cry and rushed me.

I blocked the arrow with my shield and braced myself for the oncoming fighter, the one that disappeared bothered me since he had yet to reappear. The arrow rebounded back toward the bowman, who to my surprise, caught it in his hand and re-notched the arrow all in one quick move. I had a feeling this guy did not have any fly swatters in his home. I stepped to the side which put the fighter who rushed me between the bowman and myself. I blocked a blow from his battle-axe with my shield and the backlash forced him back. I then began to swing while he was unbalanced and gained the advantage. Then, I heard the snap of the invisible fighter's whip. It wrapped around Sword, tore it from my grasp and flung it across the room. The invisible fighter reappeared at my far right.

I lost my chance to attack the fighter in front of me with Sword, but did not want to lose the chance to have a free blow so I used a front kick and caught him in the helmet before he could recover his balance. The kick knocked him off his feet, and he fell on his back. Unfortunately, he was unharmed and I quickly pulled out the Blade of Cutting.

I had kept the blade safely sheathed just in case I ever needed it and was glad I did. There was another snap and the Blade of Cutting was snapped from my hand before I even had a chance to get it fully withdrawn. I was now weaponless and my shield no longer had its unique ability. Sword was a good thirty feet from me and I knew I would have two or three arrows stuck in me before I could reach it. My situation looked hopeless, when the cavalry arrived.

I blocked an arrow with my shield but received a deep gash across my cheek from the metallic whip. The fighter on the ground rose to his feet. I kicked him in the head and knocked him down again. When a battle cry from the hall signaled others had joined the fray. The four of us stopped and turned to see which side, if any, this new addition was here to help. To my amazement and relief Glam and La'tian came into the room followed by Doc and Glum. I was filled with renewed vigor, charging the guy with the whip. Because of the speed my boots gave me, he misjudged the distance. The whip hit me before it snapped and bounced off my chest without harming me.

I jumped into the air and caught him dead in the chest with a kick; he flew backwards and slid down the wall. I turned and made a dash for Sword, running as fast as I could. I nearly ran straight into the wall in my haste to reach the all-important weapon. I took a quick glance at my surroundings before I reached for Sword to make sure I was not going to be a sitting duck. Sword was once again in my possession and I now had help, victory was within sight.

I spun and quickly assessed the situation. Glam was pressed into a corner by the monk who fought him bare handed and La'tian held her own against the warrior with the battle-axe. Doc and Glum guarded the doorway and the fighter with the whip advanced on me. I rushed him and anticipated his attack. He lashed out and I blocked it with my shield which sent the tip flying wildly back at him. I reached him before he had time to regain control of his weapon. The whip changed into a flaming sword in front of my eyes when I attacked. He blocked my blow with his shield and took a low swing at my legs. I hopped over his weapon, and at the zenith of my jump, kicked him in the helmet. My trained kick rattled his head and I brought Sword down on his shoulder plate, cutting a deep gash into it.

He lost the use of his shield arm and became easy prey to my fierce assault. I chopped wildly down on him several times while he desperately blocked with his sword. I purposely allowed him to attack so I could block with my shield thus putting his sword in a position where it would be useless to defend with. He took the bait as I planned. He nearly lost his sword from the ferociousness of his last desperate swing and the surprise rebound he received from my shield. This enabled me to stab straight into his unprotected chest plate. The warrior fell back and I wrenched Sword loose from his body.

I turned in time to see the monk snap Glum's neck. Glam was already lying in a pool of his own blood. La'tian still held the other fighter at bay while Doc growled at the human ready to try and defend against him.

"Try me next Surrean slime!"

The monk ignored Doc and nonchalantly walked my way. Either this guy was an idiot to fight a man with a sword and shield bare handed, or he was really good with his hands and feet, which was more likely since he had already taken out Glam under the same conditions.

While he approached me, he went through several moves similar to disciplines I had been taught. I felt like I was in some *B* rated Kung Fu movie. I charged him and swung Sword. He clapped his hands together and caught Sword in mid stride, twisted his wrists snatching Sword from my grasp and threw it behind him. He followed up with a sort of roundhouse sidekick to my chest that I had never seen before. I did not even have time to block. I stumbled back to catch my breath. The only way I could beat this guy was on his own ground. I tossed my shield aside and warmed up with a couple of my own moves. His eyes narrowed and a grin came across his lips.

We stood facing each other in our own individual stances, him in some sort of inverted back stance, while I stood with a front stance ready to counter his inevitable attack. He leapt into the air and spun, his foot came out of nowhere and caught me in the jaw using another strange maneuver. Luckily, I moved enough to where his blow barely caught me, but none the less it stunned me.

I stepped back to gain the time to clear my head and draw energy from inside. He pressed the attack and made the mistake of using a spinning jump kick, a move I was familiar with. I caught his leg when it came around and hit him in the crotch with a quick jab, kicked his other leg out from under him, then threw him to the ground. I tried to bring my heel down into his mid-section with a front stamping kick, but he caught the blow before it connected and threw me to the ground. We both jumped up and resumed our original stances, but he no longer grinned. Instead he had the look of pain on his face, a look I was very familiar with.

It was my turn to try some of my favorite moves on him. I leaped forward and threw a series of kicks and punches, which he blocked while countering with several of his own that I blocked. We continued this private battle, each trying new moves, one after another, until a blow finally connected. Unfortunately, it was his. He caught me in the nose with a palm, which stunned me, hit me in the solar plexus and followed up with a kick to my ribs. I went down fast and hard.

Fortunately, I was well trained in the art of pain control and found a definite need for the ability. He used some kind of weird jumping stomp kick aimed at my head and did the maneuver so quick I barely had time to avoid the blow. I was lucky I did, since he cracked the stone floor with it. I kicked him in the side when he landed, and that gave me the opportunity to regain my feet.

We both returned to our stances, but this time I used a back stance. I was not fond of this stance, but since I was fighting an unknown form of martial arts I decided it might be useful in defending against my enemy's unusual style. He wasted no time attacking. I guess since I had received the more damaging blows during our fight so far, he felt he had the advantage, which could well prove to be his undoing. I waited for his flurry of attacks, blocking each one in turn. I waited for the opening I was sure would come, found it and used a fatal blow to the throat. My move connected and took the fight out of him momentarily like I expected it would. I took advantage of his precarious position and kicked him in the crotch. I threw an elbow to his mid-section and chopped him across the throat again.

Normally I would have stopped a long time ago, but this was a fight to the death, a fight I could not lose. I followed up with clapping my hands on his ears, and then broke his knee with a solid heel kick. He went down spitting up blood and I finished the job by snapping his neck with my heel while he was on the ground.

I was so psyched up I sensed the weapon coming at my head from behind even before Doc's inaudible warning entered my mind. I kicked blindly behind me, my kick was so vicious I dented his chest plate and tossed the enormous weight a good ten feet before he touched the ground. I turned to direct my attention to a new opponent who dared make a stand against me. That was the moment I saw La'tian's headless corpse and did what all my training had taught me not to, I lost control.

There was a sword lying nearby that I thoughtlessly picked up and ran recklessly toward the object of my anger. My kick had hit so hard it had momentarily stunned him, but nonetheless he was on his feet before I could reach him. He tried to defend against my merciless attack, but to no avail. I pressed him against a wall and beat on his shield until it was battered into a deformed relic of the shiny glory it once was, and his arm was bruised and useless. During this wild attack on his armor, he tried to counter attack and nearly lost his weapon for the effort.

I began to tire and lose the bloodlust that had made me go stark raving mad when he decided to retaliate. I was now the one defending against his frantic blows, when my sanity popped back into existence. It was his undoing. I blocked his next attack, spun around and jabbed the sword into the side of his armor with all my remaining strength. The sword buried itself deep into his side and would have buried itself all the way to the hilt if it had not been stopped by his armor on the other side.

I left the sword buried deep into his side and jumped back, weaponless, ready to defend against any unforeseen attacks. None came; the fighter that I had just gutted stood motionless, like a statue from some great war, then fell over dead from my fatal blow.

The adrenaline left me and so did my legs; I collapsed to the ground exhausted. Doc ran over to me and stood guard. I felt like he was the only thing between me and obliteration. While I lay there, I tried to collect my wits; but it seemed I no longer had the strength or the will power to continue with this so-called destiny. I began to lose Sterling and was once again good old Tom Brown, who never wanted this quest I had been forced into.

Resentment coursed through every vein in my body. That horrible ring forced me into doing unforgivable things since I landed on this planet. I really could not decide if it was resentment or plain hatred. Either way I wanted nothing more to do with this place. I grabbed the ring off my finger and threw it across the room. It was not until I heard it clink across the floor that I realized it had come off and what I had done. I suddenly felt weak, hopeless and very frail. Something inside told me I had done a very stupid and ignorant thing. I no longer wanted to listen to that voice and wanted to ignore all the feelings raging inside me. Doc even seemed like good old Doc again, dumb, faithful and clumsy.

I looked around at the carnage in the room. The great dragon that laid dead and dismembered representing the power of the universe that was quickly dying. There were five dead warriors of evil, which may have actually won their battle. Glam, who was the representative of strength and courage that would eventually stumble and fall. La'tian, who represented beauty and anything that could even be considered elegant, crushed by greed and corruption.

Then there was Glum, little Glum who symbolized good everywhere, destroyed by the very evil he strived to eradicate. Last but not least, Doc and I who were left to portray the innocence of the cosmos, the ones that would truly suffer from the war between good and evil. I began to pity all of us and started to cry, one of the great abilities of the truly innocent.

Doc nudged my arm in an effort to bring me out of my little world of self-pity. I was not able to hear him as he once put it and probably would never be able to hear him speak to me again. I really had enjoyed being able to actually talk to my best friend. I would truly miss that. He looked at me with big brown eyes full of innocence. "It's alright Doc." I petted his head. "We'll just wait here for the obvious end." Doc growled and tugged on my arm. "Okay Doc, I'll follow you, what do you want?"

He started to go and turned to make sure I would follow. I got up slowly and reluctantly followed him. To my surprise he led me to Glum's twisted body and I nearly fell over when Glum spoke.

"Tom, promise me you won't give up."

"I already have Glumstron Stonefoot."

It was the first time I had ever called him by his proper name, but then I felt I owed him that.

"Then evil has already won and Glamstone, La'tian and I have died for nothing, right?"

"You always had a way with words; and you really know how to hurt a guy." I faked a smile to make him feel good in his last moments. He laughed and winced from the pain it caused.

"I want to make one final request. Will you do one thing for me?"

"As long as you don't ask me to leave here, I

will."

"Good. Remember you just gave a dying man your word. I want you to put the ring back on, hold Sword and the shield, then find the armor and put that on. Remember, you just gave me your word."

He took one final agonizing breath and died. I cried at the loss of a good friend. I looked up and saw Doc dragging Sword to me. He laid it at my feet, then spit out the ring.

"Traitor!" He stared at me and wagged his tail. I put the ring back on.

Well, can you hear me now?

Doc's voice came through crisp and clear. *I can! At least we'll have each other's company until the end comes.* I really did not mean what I said and wondered if a little of Sterling had returned. I stood then collected Sword and the shield. With each item I recovered I felt more of the sense of duty I had held before this point. The destiny that had been given to me by the forces of good pushed hard to take over. I fought this feeling; convinced Sterling would not regain a foothold in the power struggle within my ego.

I grabbed the key of Draxstill from around my neck, where it had rested safely since I gained it, walked over to a wall and placed it into a brick where it fit perfectly. It slid in and made a click letting me know it had locked into place. I did all this without thinking about what I was doing, since the Golden Dragon had not told me where the Armor of Omens was hidden.

When the brick wall magically slid open I felt like a child, wide eyed and innocent, waiting for my prize for a job well done. Finally, I would receive the spoils for the difficult Herculean tasks I accomplished. My jaw dropped from the sight of the fabulous piece of armor my weary eyes beheld. It was like staring into a void, but at the same time it was filled with brilliant colors.

The entire piece appeared to have no parts. It was an entire whole unlike any other armor made. I felt its depth was infinite, like looking into a powerful telescope at the cosmos. I was drawn into it and something inside me forced my eyes away, yet at the same time I could not stop myself from walking directly to it. I wanted to look at it again, but try as I may; I could not force myself.

It was as if the ring was protecting me from something strange and powerful within the armor, but could only protect me so much. Some unseen force guided my hand to it, and when I reached out for it my head began to swim. The moment I touched the cool metal everything went black.

CHAPTER FOURTEEN

The Final Conflict

I woke up lying flat on the ground, no longer Tom Brown. That individual no longer existed, I was Sterling the Great reincarnated and ready to fulfill my destiny. I stood up, flexed my muscles, then looked for my true companion, Bay Wolf. Looking around I found Doc. Even though Tom Brown was gone, his knowledge and training remained.

I pointed the finger with the ring on it at my longtime friend. "You will do." A blue beam emanated from my finger to strike Doc, who whimpered and was transformed into Bay Wolf.

It is good to be at your side again my old friend, I have truly missed you.

And I missed you. I laid my hand on his head. *The forces of good have need of us once again Bay Wolf, we must hurry before it's too late."* I no longer wondered who I was or what I was capable of doing. I now had full knowledge of the power and magic of the items I possessed. I was ready to battle my nemesis once and for all.

Through the insight of the Ring of Omens, I teleported us to where the last forces of the Great Southern Kingdoms were holding their war council. They were busy planning a last-ditch effort against the great evil horde that was trying to annihilate the small band of soldiers they had left. A King was speaking when I arrived so my appearance was not noticed.

"We're doomed! We don't stand a chance. They number three hundred thousand according to our last report. We are but twenty-five thousand. They outnumber us twelve to one. Asmond, where is this great savior legends speak of? If he does not arrive soon, nothing will matter anymore."

An old friend stood tall and tried to answer the king, but only found words full of doubt and uncertainty.

"Great King Hol'iton, we must take it that the evil one's interference in the realm of space and time caused the downfall of our only true hope. If that is true, we are all that is left to fight for the forces of good. We cannot give up and kneel down. If we do all is lost and we might as well all commit suicide right now. No! We must fight to the end, no matter how hopeless it is. I Asmond Hir'thito have spoken!"

A General stood. "We must try one last desperate move. I say we attack! So far, we have only been on the defensive against them. A surprise attack can catch our enemies unprepared. It may be our only hope. My soldiers are prepared to die trying!" The General slammed his armored fist down on the table.

"And if I was Sar'garian, you would all be dead." My voice bellowed from the shadows.

The twenty-one members of the meeting could not believe someone would be stupid enough to mention that accursed name and possibly give away the location of the last of the good forces, enabling *the one that could not be named* to crush his enemies in one fell swoop, all except one.

Another king stood. "Who could be so insolent as to interfere with a war council? And so dumb, or bold enough to mention that name?"

The four council guards closed in on my shadowy figure and I decided to make a grand entrance, especially since Sterling the Great always did. I teleported to the opposite side of the large tent to announce my arrival. "It is I, Sterling Justice, Sterling the Great!"

I floated in the air four feet above Bay Wolf and brandished Sword high above my head pointed toward the heavens. Twenty of them whipped around to see who I was when I first started speaking, one guard twisted his neck so fast he went to his knees in pain.

"I was worried for you old friend, but I never gave up hope!" Asmond said with a large smile across his face.

Bay Wolf growled. *The guard by the door is a spy.*

I immediately threw a stun at him to prevent his

escape, as the guard slumped to the floor unconscious. I would decide what to do with him later. Bay Wolf was never wrong.

"We don't have time for socializing old friend, right now we have a war to win and I have an abomination to destroy, later we will reminisce. The enemy is near, I feel him. He is planning a surprise attack, and we will let him make it. Of course, he will not lead the final assault, and will hide behind with his rear guard. We will be there waiting for him. He will also feel my presence and will have his most powerful soldiers there to hide behind, as pure evil always does. We still have time to plan. Generals tell your captains to hand pick their best fighters. I want the five hundred most powerful soldiers to gather at the edge of the encampment within one hour."

"Yes, Great Sterling, it shall be done!"

The General motioned to the others and they all left in response to my orders.

"Asmond, gather the most powerful wizards left, but only the ones you can positively trust. Have them gather at the same place."

"As you command old friend."

Asmond waved a hand through the air and formed an ancient symbol, then disappeared, leaving behind a small cloud of grey smoke in the shape of his body.

"Your Royal Highnesses, gather all the palace guards you have left and have them meet with the others on the outskirts of this camp. You must excuse me now. I have a few things I need to attend to."

"We shall do as you ask Champion of Good," King Hol'iton responded as each king commanded his Captain of the Guard to carry out my orders.

Once again, I called on the Ring of Omens to guide me to where Sar'garian was located and I teleported myself, Bay Wolf, and the spy posing as a council guard far away to hover high above the enemies' position.

I stunned the spy again and then tossed him to his death. Using the ability of clairvoyance, I watched the wretched soul fall and land on a soldier who stood eight feet from Sar'garian. Both men met an instant death.

I then cast an extended projected visage and my intangible image appeared before my archenemy. "Just a little present for you, *old* friend." I followed up my insult by disintegrating one of his Generals right in front of his eyes. He waived his skeletal hands with a look of wrath etched across his detestable features and disrupted my image.

I took one last look at Surrea and knew it would be completely changed within a matter of days, or even hours if I failed at the task before me. All worlds would be forever changed. Evil was destructive enough when controlled, but if it was unchallenged and allowed to go on a rampage unchecked, it always left a very ugly trail in its wake.

Only this time it was different. If I failed, there would be no good left anywhere, no pieces to pick up. I set my mind to succeed with all the determination I could muster. I knew if I fought Sar'garian on his own grounds I would lose. He had all of his forces to draw on. Three-hundred-thousand soldiers were considerably more than Bay Wolf and I could handle. Evil always hid behind the weak willed and easily controlled, but evil had weaknesses. Greed, overconfidence, corruption, and fear were its worst faults. Evil could be tricked and I planned to use all of those weaknesses against him.

I returned to all those who had gathered at my request. While the war council and I reconvened, Bay Wolf checked the soldiers as they stood at attention in their respective companies. One of his unique powers was the ability to break through any type of mental barrier. Even innate and magical defenses could not keep him from reading their minds. This made it quite easy for him to find spies.

"Generals, tell your next in command that is not gathered here to take their soldiers and attack the evil forces immediately. They are camped at Hal'ikor and are currently preparing to make a final assault on us. Go now and get everyone in place. We want to catch our enemy as unprepared as possible. Check in with me here as soon as all preparations are completed."

As the generals left, I unrolled the scroll that contained the section of land around Hal'ikor and made references to it as I spoke. "Your Royal Highnesses, we have assembled our strongest forces together, even though they only number around six hundred; they are equal in strength to ten thousand. Sar'garian will be overconfident. He will use his main force and try to crush our approaching body of soldiers when they make a frontal assault. This will considerably weaken his back lines, and that is where our main attack will happen. I need you to keep his minions busy while I confront him personally. Once he is destroyed, the mind control he exerts on the weak-minded will be severed, and that will turn the tide in our favor. The sooner I confront my nemesis, the better chance our soldiers have of surviving."

"He has spies throughout your forces and will be aware of the frontal attack; I am using this to our advantage. Right now, Bay Wolf is checking the band assembled outside for any spies. Once he has weeded them out we will be able to move without the Great Evil's knowledge, and this will give us the edge. Unless anyone has something to add, it is time to go and crush Sar'garian once and for all!"

Everybody at the war council rose, clapped and cheered before they proceeded outside. The four Generals returned from their prospective battalions and Bay Wolf and I followed behind. He found only one spy out of the five hundred and eighty-two he checked. Counting the twenty inside the tent, Bay Wolf and I brought our merry little band to a total of six hundred and three, that is after we disposed of the spy.

The small force that would attack with me from the rear began a forced march away from our main forces as they prepared for battle. I figured it would be roughly four hours before they packed up the necessary supplies and were themselves on the move. This should put us in position at just about the same time the two main forces encountered each other. We had a good thirty miles by foot in front of us and would reach our destination around midday tomorrow. I sent our best scouts out to insure our movements went unnoticed.

The first day I was informed that a small group of enemy soldiers had been detected. I personally took care of the seven sentries since I did not want any of my men destroyed and could not take the chance any of the enemy might escape. I knew they would not give me much of a problem since Sar'garian would keep his most powerful warriors at his side, now that he knew I was coming for him.

I teleported to the exterior guard post one of our scouts had found and placed a large force field around all of them to prevent any from escaping. I decapitated three of them before the rest were even aware of my presence. Then I threw a fireball at a fourth foe frying him to a crisp as the enclosed area was engulfed by a strong smell of cooking flesh while the remaining three retaliated against my attack.

One sent a lightning bolt at me that I blocked with my shield reflecting it back at him, the strong electrical current cooked him from the inside out and his smoldering body only added to the smell inside the force field boundary. I then did a back-kick at a fighter swinging a sword at my blind side and swung Sword at the last assailant, slicing clean through his mid-section, armor and all, chopping him completely in half. I turned around and disintegrated the one I had kicked before he could regain his balance. Within ten seconds after I had appeared, seven lost souls were sent to their Evil God. I dispelled my force field and teleported the bodies into deep space to eliminate all traces of a scrimmage. Satisfied all was clear I returned to my allies.

"Couldn't find them? I explained right where they were, great Sterling," the scout said.

"Easy prey, right old friend? The dangerous ones lie close to *the one who cannot be named*, don't they?" Asmond stated showing the wisdom he possessed.

"Yes, Asmond. As usual, you are correct. The seven I encountered have journeyed to meet their Evil God and will not give away our surprise rear attack. Hopefully we will be as lucky in the future."

I looked over at the scout who thought I had not found the outpost. The poor guy was beet red and evidently realized how foolish his words had sounded. "Good job soldier. If you had not located their outpost before we were spotted, all would have been lost. Keep up the good work." I hoped what I said made the young man regain his confidence and feel less foolish.

"Yes sir." He sat up in his saddle, saluted and rode away.

We traveled the rest of that day and through part of the night, without any more encounters that we knew of. Just before midnight we camped and the soldiers were informed not to light any fires. I posted twice as many guards as usual. I didn't want to take any chances this far into the game. Luckily, we spent the rest of the evening without any occurrences.

The moment the sun kissed the horizon we headed toward an unknown fate. By noon if all went right we would be in position to start the last offensive. The importance of this day weighed heavily on everyone as we marched through the morning hours and steadily drew nearer to our destination. Contemplating a negative outcome to this battle was too overwhelming to even think of. Right now, the battle was the only thing that mattered.

Our main force would have been spotted by now and Sar'garian's army would be converging on them soon. We needed to attack his back door before his main force engaged and destroyed the frontal assault or we would be overpowered by sheer numbers. As long as there was a large force attacking from his front, he would not be able to recall a large number of his soldiers. Actually, I hoped he would, because it would put a large number of soldiers out of circulation for a period of time until they reached the rear battle.

While we marched, my stomach churned and I had a feeling of impending doom. Like something had gone astray with my plans, maybe we had been spotted or possibly the two main forces were already battling and our troops would be wiped out too soon. We made it to the area I chose to base our attack from without mishap and we began to organize and set up for the assault. The Kings and their guards, the Generals and their armies, and the most powerful magicians with Asmond leading them all lined up for action, waiting for my signal. I looked over my small army one last time and the group looked like some huge parade ready to march a large city's street on New Year's Day. The colors were magnificent, several soldiers proudly held high the banners representing their kingdoms, each one full of color and beauty. The wizards wore robes of all kinds of styles, color and description. The soldiers' armor and shields were alive with symbols and crests of numerous types. There was every kind of creature normally used for transportation on this world, and a few that were not.

Everyone, from the Generals to the Privates waited for my signal. As I raised Sword up to signal them to charge into battle, I felt like the bandleader raising his baton to indicate it was time to start the music and begin marching. I hesitated for some unknown reason; it was like I felt I was sending all of them to their demise. But I pushed back these feelings knowing they were all dead anyway if we didn't succeed, so it didn't really matter. They all deserved a fighting chance and would rather die on the field with honor than hide like cowards anyway.

I hesitated no longer, Sword made the fatal swish through the air and my allies burst into action, while I teleported Bay Wolf and myself into the valley. I now stood face to face with Sar'garian and his guards. "I have come for you, Evil One!"

"You seem to be outnumbered earthling. Two against a thousand of my best troops. And this time you don't have an army standing behind you. Crawl back to your puny planet earthman, my master has promised it to me as a play toy. Your loved ones will be the first to suffer at my hands." He cackled loudly.

"Look again undead scum, it is you that should

crawl back into the worm hole you crawled out of."
The moment I finished my sentence my small army
crested the top of the hill behind me.

"Oh, you brought a few hundred sticktles with
you. But did I say one thousand? My mistake, I
meant thirty."

His tone was wicked and full of evil that
permeated everything around him. He waived his
hand around and I looked where he indicated and
saw soldiers lining the horizon all around me and
my men. We had walked into a trap, and it was
closing in on us like a spring-loaded vice.

My allies had the look of shock and
bewilderment etched across their features. Most
looked like they had already lost the battle. If it was
not for their loyalty to the four kings of the Great
Southern Kingdoms, along with their determination
to win, they would have all surrendered. They
knew, as well as I did that evil did not take captives
and has no mercy. A fight to the death was our only
alternative.

Sar'garian had to be destroyed and I needed to do
it fast if my friends and my army stood any chance
of survival. By the time I waded through the
opposition he placed between us, my friends would
be destroyed and then I would stand-alone against a
horde of evil. Eventually, even I would perish under
the overpowering numbers he hid behind. But
Asmond picked me long ago because he knew I
would not quit no matter what kind of odds were
stacked against me. The last time I beat Kaleja's
champion, the odds were in his favor, not quite this
bad, but bad enough. Even though I had become a

better fighter over the years, Sar'garian had also gained in power and experience which kept us virtually on the same level then and now. I beat him then and I would beat him now. All I had to do was get to him.

I teleported to where he had been a couple of seconds ago. I really did not expect to find him there, but I had to start somewhere. As I expected, he fled leaving a few of his guards to welcome my arrival. As soon as I appeared I was under attack, a warrior took a swing at my head with a halberd while another attacked from behind. I activated my armor's ethereal ability and blocked the halberd with my shield. The fighter's weapon flew back and out of his hands which threw him off balance.

I decapitated him and turned to face the one behind me. His weapon did not reach into the ethereal plane of existence, so it went through my armor like it was air; and that completely disoriented the poor fellow. Expecting to feel resistance when his weapon reached me and finding none threw him off balance and he got sliced through his waist and cut in half as a reward for his effort. I turned to face the other three challengers Sar'garian left for me, but to my surprise, they turned tail and ran. I had to laugh. Maybe these idiots left the water running in their bathtubs and just remembered it? Ironic, since evil always boasted and claimed it knew no fear.

I teleported in front of them, chopping the one in front of me in half before they could react. "Going somewhere gentlemen?" When the second creature made a move I sliced him down, cleaving straight through his sword and deep into his armor. I jerked Sword free just in time to block the last fighter's stroke. The fighter tried to twist away, but that allowed me to sever the wrist of the hand that held his weapon. I did a leg sweep and he hit the ground hard, nearly knocking the wind out of him. I put the tip of Sword at his throat. "Where did your wimpy master run off to, scum?"

"I don't know, I swear!"

"You have to the count of three to answer. If you tell me where he went I give you my word I will spare your life, if you don't, I *will* kill you. One…"

"I don't know, please don't kill me."

"Two…"

"He will kill me if I tell you."

"I will kill you for sure if you don't. Three…"

"He is with his rear guard at Telk'otu Bend; he is waiting for you, Sterling. You cannot win; he has something in store for you."

I kept my word and let him live. I doubted however, he would live for very long considering the amount of blood he was losing from his severed hand. I looked to see how my allies were fairing before I followed the lead I had been given. The battle had just started and was being waged all across the plains. Not many had fallen yet, but soon the plains would be littered with bodies, the quicker I found Sar'garian and destroyed him the more lives I would save.

I teleported a short distance from where I thought Telk'otu Bend was, I remembered it on the map we used to make our battle plans with and had a general idea where to go. My guess was close enough to view my objective. I decided the only way I was going to be able to keep him from running again, was to put up several barriers around him and his guards with me inside. It would take him a short time to dispel my force fields, and if I could destroy or disable the guards around him quickly enough, then he would be forced into dealing with me directly.

I turned invisible and teleported behind him. I threw up ten force fields before someone capable of seeing invisible objects spotted me. There were eight of his minions inside the barriers with us, and I hoped I would be able to take them out before he discovered and then destroyed the fields. Fortunately, he would have to disrupt them one by one and that would take some time. I knew the ones closest to him would be the strongest, and that meant the ones inside with me.

I doubted if I could destroy them all in time, but I banked on Sar'garian sticking around to help fight against me, until only one or two of his soldiers were left, then flee again. If he did as I expected and waited a little too long before he fled, I stood a chance. The last time we fought, he was over confident, I no longer had that edge, but I was also inexperienced then and had learned a lot since.

CHAPTER FIFTEEN

Earthquakes Can Ruin Anyone's Day

Our battle had lasted a day, and this time I didn't even have hours and knew I would have to use every trick I had ever learned. The task before me seemed virtually impossible, but I was not about to give up as long as there was a breath left in me.

I immediately had three very capable warriors converge on me. I took a swing at the one on my right and blocked an attack from another with my shield, while I dodged the third one's attack. Even though my armor was virtually impenetrable, there were certain things that could harm me, and I was not willing to take a chance on anything, so the less attacks that connected, the less chance I could be hurt.

The ethereal properties of it lasted a short time, and I could only use it ten times a day, so I wanted to be picky about when I utilized this special ability. Anyway, I had a whole arsenal of powers to draw from, but unfortunately, most of them had limits on duration and number of usages.

The one I swung at blocked my lethal blow with his shield and launched an attack of his own with the two-handed broad sword he easily wielded with one hand. The one I blocked with my shield was thrown off balance, and I pierced him through the chest before he could recover. I jumped back to dodge the two-handed sword aimed at my waist and kicked the third fighter in his chest plate with a side jump kick when his sword came around for a second blow.

The last two fighters in my little trap came to aid the two I was currently fighting. That left four magicians, counting Sar'garian, to deal with. I jumped into the air, stabbed at one warrior and kicked the other, then a barrage of magic projectiles came at me from the four mages. Fortunately, they were limited on the type of spells they could throw or else they would kill their own men. And even more fortunate, magic projectiles could not penetrate my armor.

The one I kicked went down with a dented chest plate, leaving only the guy with the two-handed sword to deal with momentarily. I wanted to take him out before the other three fighters were upon me. He swung his large sword as I turned toward him, crouching to dodge his attack; I jabbed straight up into his gut.

I jerked Sword out of him just in time to block another blow by one of the two new fighters that joined the fray. The one I had kicked was up and also attacking, even the one I gutted was still standing and trying his best to return the favor. Being completely surrounded by competent fighters was not my idea of having fun, so I decided to change my situation. I really didn't want to leave the spot I was in since I had several force fields blocking my back, but felt my position was becoming precarious.

I teleported behind the warrior I gutted and buried Sword in his skull before he was aware of what happened. I immediately had a barrage of attacks come at me from the mages. One threw a fireball, another cast a lightning bolt, a third tried more magic missiles, and Sar'garian hit me with a powerful stun spell. I ducked behind my shield, rebounding the lightning bolt and fireball back to their respective origins. The magic missiles, which never miss, curved around my shield to strike home, but once again my armor proved impervious to them. The stun spell however, hit me like a ton of bricks nearly knocking me out and tossed me back against the force field. I quickly recovered my wits as the three remaining fighters rushed me.

I blocked two attacks with my shield and parried the third with Sword. The lightning bolt I rebounded struck home with its full impact and knocked the mage senseless. Evidently his constitution was strong enough to take the powerful electrical charge because it did not kill him. The magician who threw the fireball was not so lucky, even though the fire it caused did not kill him immediately; it caused his robe to catch fire. He ran around completely engulfed by flames, the other three mages dodged the living bonfire like a contagious disease, evidently more concerned with me than extinguishing the flames that were killing their ally.

Eventually he ran headlong into the force field, bounced off it and fell to the ground screaming and withering in extreme agony, to finally lie still while the flames ate up the oxygen in my little trap, which was something I had not counted on. Since I was completely engrossed with my battle, I did not notice my waning air supply.

Of the two attacks I blocked with my shield, one fighter was thrown off balance, the second one used the momentum of the recoil to come around with a faster deadlier attack, which I side stepped as I used a side snapping kick against him. I parried a remarkably well-aimed blow from the one off balance and then decapitated him. I was now down to two fighters and the three magic users.

The air was quickly exhausted by the flames, which were still burning but slowly dying out. The roughly thirty-foot diameter sphere I had made was now completely filled with smoke, and there was a sickening stench from the burning flesh of the dead magician. The dwindling air supply was beginning to be felt by all when fresh air forced the smoke away. Something I had not considered that should have been apparent to me, was someone outside the barriers disrupting them, and no doubt there were several outside the force field who were capable of dispelling them.

In the blink of an eye, I went from five

opponents, to twenty-three. Four more mages, eight more warriors, two monks, two clerics, a slaver and an outlaw, all of which were Sar'garian's personal guards. Yet so far, none had proved much of a challenge, I began to wonder what the fighter I spared had meant by, "He had something in store for me." So far it had been a breeze.

I teleported behind the fighter I just kicked. I was beginning to tire, but still had plenty of strength to drive Sword clean through his mid-section, slicing him in half. Once again, a barrage of spells was cast at me as the fighters charged. I grabbed the closest warrior to me and forced him between me and four of the six spells directed at me. I watched his face show signs of pure agony when the powerful magic spells bombarded his body. Within the blink of an eye he turned into solid stone with a look of bewilderment etched across his anguished features. Possibly to stay solid granite for the coming eons and be a monument to mark the spot of the historical battle that was currently waging around us.

Two other spells hit me from behind, absorbed by my armor, so I was not even aware they had been cast. I was slightly outnumbered, so I decided to change my odds. I had several options to choose from and decided to increase my speed first, so I threw a spell of quicken on myself that caused my movements to double for a short duration. To better intensify my increased speed, I cast a spell of sluggishness in the area around me. This spell would cut the movement of the ones affected by it in half. Being limited in power, it would probably only affect a few of them, but to those few I would be moving with blinding speed.

The two closest fighters to me were the only two that seemed to be affected by my spell, since they were moving at half the speed they were previously moving at. I quickly sliced them down as they tried to stop the object of their inevitable death, but did not have a chance to.

I now had five fighters, a slaver, two monks, and an outlaw closing in on me. The two clerics and a very menacing fighter protected six mages who had huddled around Sar'garian. The fighters and the outlaw didn't worry me, it was the two monks and especially the slaver that I was concerned about. Slavers were a very nasty lot, and always had a trick or two up their sleeve.

My hasten spell lasted for only one minute, and gave me a definite advantage, which I wanted to use before it dissipated. I cut down two more fighters amidst a flurry of attacks from the fighters and magic users. The slaver, outlaw and monks stood back and let the rest keep me busy, waiting for their opening to join the fray.

The next round of spells was directed at my enemies, instead of me. Evidently, I was killing his fighters too easily, so Sar'garian must have directed his mages to improve his soldiers' abilities. Before the spells became effective, I did a three-way jump kick with such force I dented two of the fighters' helmets and knocked the third one's helmet off. All three hit the ground hard, one with his neck snapped, the other two knocked out cold.

Immediately, the two monks and slaver attacked.

The monks used flying jump kicks of their own and the slaver tossed a steel mesh net toward me. All three evidently had hasten spells cast on them since they were now matching my speed, and mine was about to run out which would make me out classed.

I teleported behind the slaver. Just before their attacks landed, I took a swing at his blind side. Sword hit an invisible barrier and jarred my arm hard. If I wasn't in a fight for my life I would have rolled on the ground with laughter, because the two monks collided in midair as the net wrapped around them. They hit the ground hard and because of the unique properties of the slaver's net, they became completely entangled in the thing with no hope of escape without outside help. I did not want the outlaw or slaver giving them this badly needed help, but I also had the mages to consider. So, I tossed an ice blizzard spell at the mages which engulfed the small group. It caused very little, if any damage, but completely obscured their view and gave me the time I needed to take care of the others.

I teleported between the outlaw and my entangled foes. He was running to their aid and found himself running straight into Sword without a chance of escape from the steel's cold bite of death. I spun and with one stab I took the monks out of the picture. I quickly teleported, this time just a couple of feet over facing the other way since I did not want to chance the slaver taking advantage of my back to him.

Just as I expected, his whip cracked in the air right where I had just stood. I immediately stabbed two of the three fighters I had kicked down, not realizing one of them was already dead from a broken neck. I blocked another attack by the slaver's whip with my shield.

The ice blizzard was gone, and so was my hasten spell. Since the slaver was moving at twice my speed now and I was tired of messing with him, I cast one of my three disintegrate spells at him and he was no longer. This left the fighter on the ground unconscious who might rejoin the fight at any time, the two clerics, another fighter being kept in reserve for some unknown reason, the six mages and Sar'garian himself.

I was once again a target, being used for target practice by the magicians and even the clerics tossed spells my direction. I noticed the last fighter standing had not moved since he had perched himself next to his master. Something bothered me about this guy, and I was sure I would find out why, the hard way. I dodged, blocked and was hit by a couple of spells as a barrage of lightning bolts, fireballs, magic projectiles, and several other spells were cast at me. One cleric even threw an earthquake, which affected all of us. Evidently in the heat of the battle he forgot to consider the consequences of his actions.

I levitated above the ground and watched a large crack open at the feet of the motionless fighter who fell into the opening. He did not even move a muscle which made him look like some great statue violently toppled from its pedestal. The ground swallowed him whole then shut back up when the quake stopped as quickly as it began.

Sar'garian became furious and yelled something

about years of work being stupidly destroyed and then turned his wrath toward the cleric who accidentally angered his master. Since absolute evil knows no mercy, the cleric's pleas were futile and probably angered him even more, since it was considered a sign of weakness.

A split second later, Sar'garian sent the cleric to his own private hell. I took advantage of our little intermission to lop off the head of the fighter that had been knocked out earlier as he slowly began to rise. Evidently the fighter or whatever it was that fell into the ground, was the surprise that the warrior I spared had referred to.

"What's the matter, Sar'garian, did the poor baby lose his toy?" I said to heckle him.

"Kill him!"

"That's all you have to say?" Evidently angered by my question, he once again disappeared, or should I say, fled? I was getting tired of chasing him around, and time was running out. I teleported into the midst of the magicians, and before they realized I was there, three of them were down. Another two hit the ground before they could retaliate against my ferocious attacks, which left the cleric and one mage. I easily dispatched the cleric, threw up two force fields around the remaining mage and myself and teleported behind him. I put his right arm behind his back, forcing his hand up to the shoulder blade and put Sword at his throat.

"Where did Sar'garian go? I don't have time to fool around, so I am giving you one chance. If you lie to me I will know it, and you will surely perish. Tell me the truth and I will let you live. You have the word of Sterling."

"I don't know, I swear!"

The tone of fear in his voice caused it to crackle and made me believe him, but I slit his throat anyway just in case he decided to rejoin the war. I surveyed the carnage from the hilltop I was perched upon. The battlefield below was strewn with bodies of the dead and dying. Even though my friends and allies were completely outnumbered, nearly half of them still stood.

They were giving the evil horde a gallant fight. There were around five thousand bodies scattered on the ground, already showing an unequaled fierceness with which my side was fighting. But they battled to no avail since there was a good twenty-five thousand against a mere three hundred. They were about to be over-run.

CHAPTER SIXTEEN

Trick or Treat or Go'lithum

Just when I felt time had run out to save my friends, a virtual forest crested the hill in front of me, an army of ten thousand Tre'tons had joined the crusade. Being very powerful beings, their presence turned a hopeless situation into a fighting chance in the twinkling of an eye. The tide just turned in our favor. At the front leading the Tre'ton army was a golden dragon!

I rubbed my eyes in disbelief, because perched on top of the dragon was Glum, Glam and La'tian! A little of Tom Brown surfaced, as my heart jumped for joy. Never had I felt this happy to see anyone, let alone three people I had grown to love. A strength I had never experienced before welled inside me. I was ready to take Sar'garian out of existence forever.

The ring caused my gaze to be drawn to a cliff that overlooked the entire battlefield and perched on top of it was Sar'garian and only one other. I found him! I teleported there and looked into the emotionless eyes of my nemesis for what I hoped was the final battle. I was determined not to allow him to run again. This time there were only two of them to deal with, I put up a couple of force fields around us to deter his escape.

"You can no longer run, Sar'garian, your destiny has caught up with you." As I talked I kept throwing up force fields, there were now fifteen in place.

"First you must get past my friend here, Sterling the Meek!"

He gave an evil chuckle as I put a few force fields around his minion leaving just the two of us to battle each other.

Sar'garian looked at his servant and pointed a skeletal finger at me. "Kill him!

I started towards Sar'garian, when to my surprise the armored fighter spurred into action and walked right through my force fields as if they were not even there. I heard the whirl of mechanical machinery when his visor slid up to show a mirrored surface that protected his eyes. Beams of energy shot out from the mirrored area. I instinctively dodged the first blast, which struck the ground and blocked the second blast with my shield.

To my dismay, the Shield of Omens that was supposed to repel all forms of energy did not repel this warrior's beam. I was knocked back against my energy field and I felt like someone had hit me in the head with a baseball bat. Another blast came my way, and I did not want to see how many blasts I could handle before they knocked me unconscious, so I dodged it. That one beam disrupted every force field I had put up around us.

I teleported behind the peculiar fighter and brought Sword down on its head, Sword bounced off the unusual metal barely scratching it. That was the first time the Sword of Omens failed to cut through anything other than a force field. He turned around and hit me bare fisted in my chest plate. I flew about ten feet in the air and landed flat on my back.

The wind had been knocked out of me, and I tried to catch my breath as the fighter walked toward me. For the first time since its creation, the Armor of Omens had been damaged. It now had a large dent the size of the warrior's fist, pressing against my chest, right where the fighter had clobbered me.

All three Items of Omens seemed to be useless against this fighter, and I doubted if any of the magic I could toss at it would have any kind of effect. To make matters worse, I dropped Sword when he struck me and without it I lost a considerable amount of my power, including the ability to teleport which was the only means of escaping my inevitable destruction.

"How do you like my metallic man, Sterling? His name is Go'lithum. I found a scroll mentioning his powers and it gave clues on how to find and control him. It took me four long years of searching, until I found him and this…."

Sar'garian held out a metallic box made out of the same metal as the warrior closing in on me.

"Is the only thing that can control him. You luckily didn't have to fight the android I had Go'lithum design especially for you. That imbecilic cleric ruined my fun, but I still plan to have fun with you before I kill you. Watching you writhe in pain will be entertaining." He laughed.

He laughed even louder when the metallic warrior picked me up and threw me twenty feet to smash against a boulder, luckily the armor protected me from the majority of the blow, but it still rattled my brain. While I caught my breath the metallic fighter once again moved slowly toward me.

"He is from another time and dimension. His kind is unknown in our universe and because of this metal box, I am the only being in existence he will listen to. Go'lithum stop, it's my turn to play with our friend."

The thing came to a complete standstill and the visor once again closed. When out of nowhere, Bay Wolf flew through the air and headed straight for Sar'garian. He clamped his teeth on the metallic box and snatched it out of Sar'garian's hand. Sar'garian yelled in anguish and cast a spell at Bay Wolf while I used telekinesis on Sword, one of the few spells I could still cast. Sword flew through the air and was once again in my hand. Sar'garian was so entranced with recovering his control over Go'lithum he did not even notice I once again held the Sword of Omens.

I teleported behind Sar'garian and swung with all

my might at his neck. Within a split second it was over. I severed the neck of the greatest evil this world had ever known. His body stood there as if it was unaware it had lost its head. It wobbled, then slumped to the ground. He turned to a pile of ashes right before my eyes. All I could do was stare as a gust of wind hit the pile and scattered the ashes everywhere.

I looked over at Bay Wolf lying there, a true champion who gave his life to save mine. My heart ached for an old and trusted friend. His loyalty and courage just saved everyone. Had it not been for him grabbing that box I do not know what I would have done. There was a good chance that evil may have won. I sat next to him and petted his head, silently thanking him for what he had done.

Just as quick as Sar'garian had disappeared, so did Sterling the Great and his faithful companion, Bay Wolf, to be replaced once again by my true identity Thomas Brown. I now stared at my best friend who laid motionless on the grass. Just then a spark of life reared itself in his limp frame. I had a tear in my eye and ignored the raging battle below. Doc took a breath and began to move his legs. He raised his head, opened his eyes and looked at me.

We did it Tom; I remember everything that has happened.

Yes Doc, Sterling and Bay Wolf did a fantastic job. I also remembered everything that had transpired.

Amazing was all I could think. The battle was nearly won and the evilest creature to ever exist anywhere was just destroyed, no more to terrorize this planet, or any other. However, my men did not know the news. I wanted to shout from the mountaintop the elation of victory. I wanted to share with all the people of good the reclamation of their lives, and that they no longer had to fear evil, at least for now. There would be a celebration soon enough. Right now, there was a battle to finish.

Doc slowly regained his strength and we went to the edge of the twenty-foot cliff to view the battle waging below. The tide had turned completely against the evil forces. Over half of Sar'garian's troops had been hypnotized or forced into fighting for him, and now that he was destroyed, the hypnotic spell was broken. These men either fled or turned on the true evil forces. The numbers had switched from my eight thousand remaining allies against their twenty thousand to sixteen thousand on the side of good against maybe ten thousand evil forces that were left.

I grabbed Go'lithum's control box, there were no controls, switches or levers visibly apparent on its smooth surface. I figured it must be some sort of mental link with the metallic man. I tried out my guess.

"Go'lithum, come here." He responded flawlessly to my verbal command.

"Can you speak?"

"Yes." A metallic voice was heard in response to my question.

"Can you detect evil?"

"Does not compute."

"Can you determine which soldiers are fighting for which side, out of the fighters that are battling down there?" I pointed at the battlefield.

"Define side."

Evidently Go'lithum had a computerized mind, so I did my best to give him the definition of *side*.

"Unable to make a decision to which side soldier is on, there is too much of a variance in raiment and equipment to make a valid decision."

Doc wait here. "Go'lithum protect this animal from harm, but only use force if necessary. Do you understand?"

"Yes."

I left Doc in Go'lithum's care and teleported down to help defeat the waning forces of evil. News of Sar'garian's death spread through their lines like wildfire. It was plain to see that many of them could no longer feel the evil that had controlled them, so more and more soldiers fled. Within a couple of hours all the enemy soldiers were either destroyed or had run off.

During those last hours I ran across Glum, who was busy healing the wounded.

"How is it that you, Glamrock, La'tian and Omens are alive and here?" I was still amazed because I know they died. I had no doubt in my mind.

"I don't know. I floated through a black void, a magnificent voice told me to follow the light. Once I entered the light that I could not resist, the voice told me it was not my time yet. The next thing I knew I was standing in front of a Tre'ton army with Glamrock, La'tian and the Golden Dragon named Omens. All three of them said the same thing happened to them."

We gathered our forces, left a group to take care of the dead and wounded, and made a forced march to where the two main forces should still be battling. We were fourteen thousand strong and hoped we were in time to save our remaining forces. There should have been roughly two hundred and seventy thousand against our twenty-four thousand in the beginning, about two hundred and sixty thousand should have been left when Sar'garian was destroyed. We figured at least half of them would have run or switched sides when the hypnotic trance was severed, that left about a hundred and thirty thousand of his loyal troops left. There were probably around eight to ten thousand of our allies left when this happened, and we hoped that forty to eighty thousand sided with them out of anger from being made into slaves by the evil sorcerer.

According to the troops that had joined our side after being released from their enchanted state, we were half a day's march by foot from the main battle. Since most of our mounts had been lost, we were forced to go at the pace of the slowest soldier in our ranks. So, we decided to split into three groups.

Those that could teleport themselves, along with however many they could include due to the limitations of each one's proficiency at casting the spell, would go ahead and join the battle immediately. In this way we would raise the spirits of our troops to know help was on the way. Second, the fighters that still had mounts would ride ahead of the foot soldiers, so our cavalry would arrive in three separate groups. The first group, of which I was one, was comprised of one hundred of our strongest warriors, wizards, clerics and various other professions. The second group to arrive was two thousand strong, and the remainder would arrive about four hours after the second group did, nearly twelve thousand strong.

Through the directions of a tracker, the first group teleported together to the same spot overlooking the area the evil horde would use to ambush our unwitting force. We viewed a scene of great carnage where eighty to a hundred thousand bodies littered the battlefield. The battle still raged, and it was impossible to tell how many of our forces remained, and how many were against us. There looked to be around a hundred and fifty thousand troops still standing.

"I wish there was some way we could know which ones ours were."

Asmond shook his head. "If we teleport down to the center of the battle, stay in a group and attack only the ones attacking us, eventually our troops will rally around us." Once again showing his wisdom.

We all agreed it was our best course of action. I tied to bring Go'lithum with me, but he was not there when I appeared. Perplexed by this, I told Asmond I would be right back. I returned to where our group had originally teleported from and I found Go'lithum standing right where he had been when I cast the spell.

After questioning the robot and trying a few experiments, I finally came to the conclusion that magic would not work on the metallic man. So, I had Go'lithum climb onto a chariot with instructions to follow the driver's commands until he was once again in my presence.

When I returned I noticed the group had teleported to the middle of the battleground and were being attacked. Making my way back to Asmond in the center of the battlefield, I once again found myself having to fight as one enemy after another attacked me. They were everywhere, but they were not as inspired as they once were. A feeling of Evil still lingered, but it was not as strong as it had been when Sar'garian was still alive.

As the day progressed, our small circle continued to grow. We now had a good twenty thousand inside when the second wave appeared. After giving Go'lithum the command to come to me, I watched him march across the battlefield without being accosted, since no one from either of the main groups knew which side the robot was on. Once he was by my side I told Go'lithum to attack only the ones that attacked anyone in our group, he responded in his usual logical manner that he understood and stated he would comply with the order.

I once again braced myself for the warriors running toward me, but as quick as one decided to advance on me, there was a large hole in his chest. Warrior after warrior met the same fate, and I looked over at Go'lithum. He blasted one then another hostile fighter that dared to attack our group. He not only blew away fighters coming at me, but every fighter that threatened our section of the circle, and he did so with extreme accuracy. I told him to stay by Doc and continue protecting our group while I teleported to the opposite side of our ever-growing circle so I would have a chance to fight somebody.

Commands were given throughout the troops and our circle of death began to slowly drift across the battlefield toward the cavalry that finally arrived. The enemy retreated and reformed their lines which allowed our troops to rally also. There were forty thousand of our soldiers lining one side of the mile-long stretch of plains that had served as our death filled war zone, with seventy thousand facing us on the opposite banks.

I sent Go'lithum walking across the field with orders to destroy the enemy army. As innocent as a child, and as deadly as an unexploded bomb waiting to be goaded into going off, he nonchalantly walked toward the enemy lines.

We waited for the attack that never came, to my horror and surprise, Go'lithum went half way across the field, stopped and began to destroy about a hundred enemy troops a second with a wide energy beam shot in quick random spurts. Sar'garian had been so sure of his victory in battle and so worried about Sterling, he never realized the power he possessed. This one robot was capable of destroying entire armies and could have easily handed Sar'garian an undisputed victory over the forces of good. If he would have used it to destroy our armies instead of holding it in reserve to destroy just one man, he would surely have won the war.

The few remaining enemy wizards in their quickly diminishing ranks, tried to retaliate against the metallic man, and were fried for their efforts. One sorcerer even threw a large force field in front of Go'lithum and found out the hard way, just like I did, about how effective force fields were on him. Within a minute and a half, ten thousand enemy soldiers were destroyed where they stood.

Their ranks were completely broken. The Generals tried to maintain order, but to no avail. Rumors of Sar'garian's death, and one enemy soldier killing so many of their comrades so quickly, was more than they could handle. The remaining enemy forces found it too much for them and they scattered in all directions except one, toward us. They ran from us, and Go'lithum followed slowly blowing away thousands while they tried to escape his lethal blasts of energy. The enemy scattered into the hills. Then a deafening victory cheer echoed across the land. Evil was defeated.

We had won!

CHAPTER SEVENTEEN

To Be King or Not to Be King, That Is the Question

We were combing the battlefield looking for the living while the clerics brought back to life those they could, as an unneeded army of foot soldiers hurriedly came upon the battle scene.

The next couple of weeks were comprised of burying the dead and giving each the funeral rites of their own private beliefs. Next came the rebuilding of the kingdoms that had been destroyed by the evil hordes, although it would take years to complete.

Everyone worked together in the beginning to help rebuild. Even kingdoms that were normally at war with each other worked side by side without mishap. The plans made by the kings that joined together at Kal'ijora, which was later known as the Great Reconstruction Council, decided to help the kingdoms that were the most damaged first. Each kingdom was rebuilt until they were fit enough to support the essentials of life. When the workers left, the kingdom was given back to the respective ruler and his people to finish the necessary reconstruction of the cities, towns and castles.

After the Great Reconstruction Council disbanded, plans had been made to have the greatest victory feast in history. It was so large it had to be held outside in the plains of Kal'ijino, next to the great city of Kal'ijora. There was not an enclosure in existence that could house the over eight hundred thousand peasants, warriors, citizens, travelers, creatures, and royalty that attended.

It was a feast of such great magnitude that it had never been seen before, nor would it probably ever be seen again. Magicians performed magic feats to amaze and astound the multitudes, court jesters competed with each other in contests of comedy. Jugglers, acrobats, wrestling matches, and jousts of all types were held. The feast lasted for eight days, and at the end of it, ceremonies were held in honor of the soldiers that had died and those that had performed acts of great heroism. Sir John of Xant was given a sword of pure platinum for risking his life to save his king against much greater odds. A warrior named Tir Harn of the Red Clan was awarded a large piece of land in the Hil'stik region for leading a charge to rescue the four Great Kings and their guards from sure destruction.

Glum sat beside me during the eight days of the Great Feast. He explained that this land automatically made the warrior a baron and was possibly the greatest honor given. Many other brave soldiers were honored, even Glum and Glam were given awards. The ceremonies lasted almost four days when King Hol'iton stood up and raised his hand to silence the crowd.

"Now, for the last and greatest heroes to be honored here..." He yelled as loud as he could. "If it wasn't for this great warrior and his companion, none of us here would be alive today. Their tale shall be told for centuries to come by story tellers in every land and will live forever in the hearts of all good men. Sterling the Great and Bay Wolf, approach me."

I was once again called on to be Sterling. *Just this one last time* I thought to myself *and then I can be good old Tom for the rest of my life.*

Doc growled. *Sure, just think of yourself. At least you look like Sterling, Bay Wolf wasn't half as good looking as I am!*

You're just jealous you aren't the magnificent beast Bay Wolf is!

I think it's Bay Wolf who is jealous of me!

I laughed and so did Doc as we walked to the podium laughing all the way. *Doc, get serious and enjoy your moment of glory.* We walked up the steps and I knelt before the Great King and bowed my head as I had seen all the others do. Doc sat and bowed his head. The King placed something on my head then spoke.

"Rise King Sterling of Has'ilon, you above all others have proven the right to bear this title."

I started to argue the point, but decided it might be considered rude or an insult. Besides, who in their right mind would turn down their own kingdom? I started to think I might like living on Surrea for the first time since I woke up in the dark at Horzule's Keep. Yet I knew I belonged back in the good old U.S.A. on mother earth. Besides, I missed my friends and family dearly, but I had been on Surrea for a couple of months. What would another month or two matter? I could return whenever I wanted. At least I thought I could. This was not the time to ask. I decided to be King for a short time at least. Besides I deserved it considering what I had been through.

Over the next couple of weeks, I helped rebuild the kingdom of Has'ilon. The former royal family and all of its heirs had been killed during the war. Glum became my royal advisor, I made Glam the General of my growing army, and I took a bride, the Great Queen of Has'ilon, Queen La'tian.

I commanded Go'lithum to protect her, and he became her personal body guard. Wherever she went, he followed and she quickly became known as the most protected queen in the universe, since he never left her side even when she slept or bathed. Asmond became the Court Sorcerer of Has'ilon, and Omens was given the title of castle guardian, and given the task of guarding the Items of Omens.

Peasants, citizens, and soldiers of kingdoms that had been totally destroyed by the evil horde, and mercenaries that had heard of my great deeds flowed into Has'ilon. Within a couple of months, I had built a kingdom that rivaled the Great Southern Kingdoms. It was a lot of work and not at all what I expected. Being a king and running a kingdom was boring and tedious. It was nothing like the glamour one would expect. If it was not for La'tian and my other friends, I would have left Surrea and returned to Earth a long time ago.

After three months of building my kingdom I finally decided to return to my native home. Asmond foresaw this and prepared a powerful magical item for me as a going away gift. It was a ring, even more beautiful than the Ring of Omens, which I had put away in the castle treasure room along with the other Items of Omens, long ago. He told me the ring would bring me back to Has'ilon anytime I wanted, all I had to do was say "take me to Has'ilon" and poof, I would be there.

It was the perfect gift and I thanked him for it. I then said goodbye to all my dear friends and especially my wife. I wiped away her tears and kissed her luscious lips. "I'll be back, I promise I'll see you soon, my dearest. Take care of our kingdom until I return, I will always love you."

I felt like I had lied to her because I really did not know if I would ever come back to this strange world I had grown to love. Somehow, deep in my gut, I knew I would be back one way or another.

I said my final goodbyes, kissed my lovely La'tian one last time and motioned to Asmond to send us back before I changed my mind. He waived his hand and darkness engulfed me.

CHAPTER EIGHTEEN

To Dream the Impossible Dream

I awoke feeling a large wet tongue lick my face. I opened my eyes to see Doc in front of an old familiar scene. I was lying in my bed, in my bedroom, in my home back on good old mother earth. I sat up and looked around as the events of the past several months swept over me. Was it all a dream, or did it really happen? It was all so real, I remembered every second. Now I knew how Dorothy felt when she returned from the Land of Oz.

"It couldn't have been all a dream, could it Doc?" The phone rang; a sound I felt I had not heard in a very long time. "Hello?"

"Mr. Brown?"

"Yes?"

"This is J. Q. Morton. You asked me to do a

complete genealogy of your family a couple of months ago?"

The statement, "a couple of months ago" bothered me, but then a couple was a figure of speech. It could mean two on up, but I had to know. My clock said July 2nd, but I didn't want to believe it. "What's the date?"

"Excuse me sir?"

"The date, today's date?"

"Why, it's Saturday the second."

"The month?" I knew that question sounded peculiar, but I had to know. I started to feel excited.

"It's July. Why do you ask?" Mr. Morton laughed. "I guess you thought it was still June?"

If he only knew. "Yeah, I did. Sorry. Guess I got confused." I couldn't believe his answer, it was the day after I found the ring! "What did you find out about my ancestry?"

"Nothing extraordinary, except this might interest you. Around 1200 A.D. there was a duke whose family had a great deal to do with the formation of the knights of the round table and helping Arthur gain his kingdom. This duke was part of your family tree and was considered very powerful according to the literature I dug up on him. But he vanished at the height of his power and was never seen again."

"What was his name?" I could hear the man thumbing through papers

"Uh, Sterling, Sterling Justice."

"Thank you..." I was in a daze as I hung up the phone without thinking.

A thought occurred to me and I snapped out of

my confused state. The ring. I looked at the piece of metal on my finger, and as I expected, it was not the Ring of Omens, it was the one Asmond gave me. I tried to remove it to inspect it better but I would not budge, I couldn't even twist it around on my finger. It was like it was part of my finger.

All my memories could not be a dream. Had I gone through some sort of a psychic phenomenon? If it was a dream, how did I end up in my bed wearing a completely different ring than the one I originally found? Did I dream I found a different ring? And how would I have known the name of my ancestor? That is not a name I had ever heard before.

Confusion in my case was perfectly normal. Normal? What happened to me could never be considered normal! Falling in love with the woman of my dreams in a dream? That sounds insane, but I believed it to be true. I decided it best not to think about Kings, and especially not to think about evil in the worst possible form. Fighting wars, beheading people and doing unspeakable things. Who would believe any of my stories? I had trouble believing them and I was there!

Of course, I held to the belief that my adventures in Surrea were real and Asmond had sent me back in time when he sent me home. That had to be it, even if it was illogical. The more I thought the more confused I became. I needed a drink. A really strong one.

I went into the kitchen and found the broken bottle on the counter where I left it. I let Doc out and went to take a shower; I walked into the bathroom and stopped dead in my tracks. I backed up and looked into the mirror to make sure that what I thought I had seen out of the corner of my eye was what I saw. My jaw dropped, for in the mirror was my naked body, covered with scars from the numerous wounds I received on Surrea and they were all completely healed. It wasn't a dream, it had been real, all of it. These scars were proof positive of what I went through and accomplished.

Each scar had a story to tell and I was proud to have been a part of such an exciting and worthy experience. Plus La'tian. Just thinking about her made my heart swell with a love like no other. She truly was my other half, the love of my life. She was beautiful, smart, loving. She completed me. How could I possibly not think about her? And Glum and Glam, I could have never finished such a difficult herculean task without them.

So many memories, I ran a finger over the rings metal. I could return at any time as long as I had this ring. But of course, I wouldn't…or would I?

The End?

ABOUT THE AUTHOR

Born in Fresno, CA but raised in San Jose, CA, Neal Petersen's writing style was inspired by J. R. R. Tolkien. After being introduced to 'The Hobbit', required reading in the ninth grade, Petersen decided he wanted to try his hand at creating his own stories.

At an early age, Neal visited his brother and two sisters in the beautiful Ozarks. He attended college at MSU in Springfield, MO, where he still resides today.

Between the ages of nineteen to twenty-one, Petersen played many hours of Dungeons and Dragons. The game, along with Tolkien, inspired his stories.

He has written everything from short stories to novels, but his favorite has always been his creation, SURREA. The original story was written in 1990 and has taken twenty-seven years to get published. It's been a long, arduous journey.

Doc was the best dog Neal ever had. He still misses him.